CW00696901

Hidden gods: the doorway

A metaphysical thriller in which two journalists in an attempt to discover
who or what is really behind the chaos in the Middle East spin back
through time to discover the secret codes of Atlantis. Their search for
the grail begins with a night in the King's chamber of the Great Pyramid
of Giza . . .

International news photographer Hugo Fitzroy, his schizophrenic son
Brent and writer Philipa Neville, have one vision in common – a great
pyramid through whose portal shines a giant sunbeam. Inside, a
miraculous escape is planned. Outside, planet earth is changing
frequency.

Against a background of the international intrigue surrounding the
Gulf War and its aftermath, the visionary trio not only discover that they
are being drawn inexorably towards the greatest secret the Middle East
has ever kept, but also towards their own destinies. For Hugo, Brent and
Philipa have loved before, in other powerful identities, and now they
have to come to terms with this as well as their responsibilities to the
hidden gods.

Also by Anthony Masters

FICTION

A pocketful of rye (1964)
The sea horse (1966)
A literary lion (1968)
Conquering heroes (1969)
The donor (1970)
The syndicate (1971)
The dead travel fast (1971)
The emperor on ice (1973)
Birds of a bloodied feather (1974)
Red ice (with Nicholas Barker, 1986)
Rig (with Nicholas Barker, 1990)
Murder is a long time coming (1991)
Confessional (1993)
Death's door (1995)

NON-FICTION

The summer that bled (1972)
Bakunin (1974)
Bedlam (1977)
Rosa Lewis (1977)
Inside marbled halls (1979)
Nancy Astor (1981)
The man who was M (1984)
Literary agents (1987)
The Newall murders (1995)

CHILDREN'S FICTION

Badger (1986)
Streetwise (1987)
Dream palace (1988)
Frog (1989)
Mel's run (1989)
Nobody's child (1989)
All the fun of the fair (1989)
Cat burglars (1989)
Siege (1990)
African queen (1990)
Shell shock (1990)
Nightmare in New York (1990)
Battle for the badgers (1990)
Sad song of the whale (1990)
Dolphin's revenge (1990)
Monsters on the beach (1990)
The song of the dead (1990)
The seventh stream (1990)
Travellers' tales (1990)
Playing with fire (1990)
Gorilla mountain (1991)
Vanishing point (1991)
Klondyker (1991)
Traffic (1991)
Crab (1992)
Tunnel terror (1992)
The transformation of Jennifer Howard (1992)
Scary tales to tell in the dark (1992)
Dead man at the door (1992)
Raven (1993)
Bullies don't hurt (1995)

HIDDEN GODS
The doorway

———

Anthony Masters

and

Hugh Colmer

Constable · London

First published in Great Britain 1995 by Constable & Company Ltd
3 The Lanchesters, 162 Fulham Palace Road, London W6 9ER
Copyright © 1995 by Anthony Masters and Hugh Colmer
The right of Anthony Masters and Hugh Colmer to be
identified as the authors of this work has been asserted
by them in accordance with the Copyright, Designs and
Patents Act 1988
ISBN 0 09 473280 9
Set in Linotron Baskerville 11pt by CentraCet Ltd, Cambridge
Printed in Great Britain by St Edmundsbury Press Ltd
Bury St Edmunds, Suffolk

A CIP catalogue record for this book
is available from the British Library

PROLOGUE
The Burning

Brent Fitzroy hated the male nurse more than he could ever show or say, and much of his time was devoted to planning a mercilessly slow death for him. Whether Gerald Paxton was being bright and breezy, authoritarian, confidential, commiserating or 'taking him seriously' – the attitude he could least endure – Brent's anger and sense of despair quickened each day.

'How's the journal going?' had been the first comment this morning as he was helped to rise from his bed – a process that he found incredibly painful. To leave the source of visionary guidance was bad enough, to be jollied out of it at the same time was unbearable.

The fact that the routine had been going on for many years did nothing to diminish its hateful intensity.

'Didn't see you writing yesterday?' said the sandy-haired, freckled Paxton, who thought he owned him.

'At least he's interesting and industrious,' he had overheard him telling the shrink. 'The pick of the bunch.' Interesting and industrious? He would like to channel all that alleged energy into attacking Paxton with a pickaxe, chopping him into small pieces and boiling them up for dog meat. It was an ambition frustrated only by the lack of the right equipment.

Half an hour later, Brent was sitting at his table in the dayroom with the sun pouring in, catching grey stubble on a withered cheek here, a bleary and bloodshot eye there, the fixed stare of

[5]

the catatonic or the chattering restlessness of the demented. He knew where he was all right – in the nut-house – and he knew why. Brent heard voices, saw visions and clouds of impending disaster hovering over the earth, knew he was Thoth, was responsible for creating Atlantis and was now receiving guidance about how to release the Atlanteans from the Great Pyramid of Giza. All this guidance had been transmitted to his journal for the benefit of his fellow revenants, but the trouble was that the instructions were not coming at him thick and fast but through a haze of intermittent reception and understanding. He could not exactly comprehend what they were telling him, although even a few months ago he had heard and seen with crystalline clarity. This was the first time in years that he had not seen his own history unfolding, and his constant torment was that the transmissions would become fainter, more obscure, and it would be less possible to commit them to his journal.

Could cornflakes be literally ground in the teeth and then intermittently spat into a finger bowl? That was what Peggy Dart did – or attempted to undertake each and every morning. Mountainous, wheezing, overburdened by her own blubbery weight, Peggy tried to induce a slimmer her by selective eating. In the mistaken belief that small meant beautiful, she chewed the cornflakes down to acceptably tiny swallows, while other pieces, mysteriously but meaningfully selected, were spat out, limp and milky, into the growing pile in the finger-bowl – or on to the stained tablecloth, if in her voracious enthusiasm she missed. He had sat opposite Peggy for over six years. But even she, with her selective appetite, was not as bad as Gerald Paxton. Brent would like to be selective by eating Paxton. He would like to hear his bones crunch.

Eventually settled at the desk in the library, he tried to remember, and wrote unsatisfactorily fractured notes in his journal. They were clumsy, insubstantial, and of little use to his future companions.

'Glad to see you back at work.' Paxton stood in the doorway, the sunlight catching his sandy hair, helping the intruder. Brent did not reply.

'What's today's adventure?'

'Piss off!'

'Now – remember what we said at yesterday's group meeting. About sharing freely but with courtesy?' His look was friendly, intense, and he was obviously eager to kick about a problem or two.

'Piss off,' repeated Brent.

He wrote painstakingly:

The Law of Reincarnation

Christianity embraced reincarnation for three hundred years before the Emperor Constantine declared it a sin. When the early Christians asked Christ whether he was Elijah who had come before, they were thinking of reincarnation. Christ said, 'Unless a man is born again, he cannot enter the kingdom of Heaven.'

In accepting reincarnation one also accepts the law of compensation, karma, i.e. carrying from one life over to another.

We return a stepping stone instead of a stumbling block. There is nothing left to chance in the Universal Grand Design; reincarnation is an instrument, not an end in itself.

The soul is not lost; only its individuality.

The real purpose of reincarnation is the message of Love.

The times of reincarnation vary according to the state of development of the individual, and to the manner and character of their removal from the material experience. As to their colour, race or sex, this depends upon the experience necessary for the completion.

One incarnation naturally merges into another. 'As the tree falls, so does it lie,' said the Maker and Giver of Life. So does the Light, so does the nature of the Individual. The beginning in the next experience is tempered by the sincere purpose of the individual in the life before.

By developing spirituality, we develop the faculty for recollection. When the purposes of the individual are in

[7]

accord with purpose, then the soul may remember what it was.

Nature does not forget; only man forgets.

But he couldn't afford to forget. There must be a way through what appeared nowadays to be the static, the blur, the unresonant, the blank screen of his originally fertile, receptive mind.

Though modern theology spurns reincarnation, it has long been considered part of the Eastern religions.

Ashes to ashes and dust to dust was not spoken of the soul. It is generally considered if a man lives again, it is his soul that lives. The Bible has many references to rebirth. The Master said, 'Ye must be born again.' He repeated it many times and confirmed to Nicodemus, 'The wind bloweth where it listeth, and thou hearest the sound thereof, but can't tell whence it cometh, and whither it goeth. So is everyone that is born of the Spirit.' He also said that John the Baptist was the reincarnation spiritually of Elias. The disciples asked Jesus, 'Who did sin, this man or his parents, that he was born blind?' And Jesus answered, 'Neither has this man sinned, nor his parents; but that the works of God should be manifest in him.'

How is it that some people we meet feel immediately familiar whilst for others we have known for years in this life we still feel no intimacy?

Thoth the Atlantean materialized on earth approximately one and a half million years ago. His origins are said to be extra-terrestrial and he is a reincarnate.

Thoth was able to communicate by thought and was able to disassemble and reassemble the atoms and molecules of objects and transport them from one place to another.

Thoth took the offspring of the Lemurians, Orions and Marduk to an island continent called Atlantis where they began to build a highly advanced technological civilization. Thoth and his scientists created a crystal so finely chiselled that it could absorb the sun's rays and create a new form of energy. Using the crystal they built a huge pyramid in the capital, Poseidon, now seen on the back of the American dollar as the all-seeing eye.

And the all-seeing eye sees nothing but blind judgement which is in accord with one molecule's mounting of action which can only become a corncrake's eye at best. On the Isle of Tiderace there barnacle heaven –

He knew he was writing nonsense – knew with heavy fatalism that he might always be writing nonsense. His third eye suffered from astigmatism, had the blinds down.

Paxton came back into the library at the worst possible moment, pushing the medication trolley as silently and as 'discreetly' as he could so as not to 'disturb' him. But it was this very earnest discretion that was the greatest disturbance of the day. Fuck him, Brent thought bitterly.

'Come on, old son. Have your pill.'

'One day – '

'One day my prince will come,' grinned Paxton, all merry and bright and full of liberal understanding. Brent could hear him saying to someone at home, 'I try and get on with them all, you know. I take them at face value.'

'Why don't – '

'Have your pill.'

Brent grabbed it and returned to scribbling nothing at all – until Paxton pushed his trolley away, preferably into some deep abyss, to burn in hell fire.

The nurse was replaced by old Cole. Cole had been at St Clouds forever. Cole talked continuously and spent much of his talking time in the library. But Brent did not mind; he was able to live and write with his gabble, all of which related to a number of imaginary bus routes which he connected and disconnected in regular geographic complexity. He had his hands permanently enclosed in padded gloves because if he could not remember a route to his entire satisfaction, he would injure himself.

'The 4, the 2, and the 3 produce the sum of nine, which is the natural number of man and also the lower worlds. The 4 represents the ignorant man, the 2 the intellectual man, and the 3 the spiritual man. If the no. 16 were the no. 28 it would go by

[9]

way of Barniton, stopping at Honeysetts, Great Lichens, Argos, Two Drains and the River Crossing. But if the 28 were the 14 or better still the big one – the 19 – for Greyshott then it's sand-dunes all the way up to the island and first stop the cliff road where it might be the no. 16.'

Brent looked up curiously. This was different from his usual spiel which was so familiar it was Muzak all the day and most of the night.

'Number 16 will run up to the first stop. Pyramid Halt.'

'What?'

Old Cole stopped in mid-sentence, amazed at a revolutionary interruption.

'Did you say pyramid?'

He looked at Brent astounded. There was going to be a conversation. 'Pyramid Halt and into the Giza. Up to Atlantis garage and route terminated. But if that route becomes a no. 14 and divides into no. 16's territory – ' He shambled slowly out of the room while Brent received an intriguing thought. If the old man was a transmitter – no, a reflector of his visions, or had only temporarily become a reflector – then what was the message? He saw again the habit the old man had got into, of holding his padded gloves aloft. Now what did that mean – for there was clearly a message in everything. Could it mean that if his own transmitter had become disconnected there was only one solution? To shock it back into action? To use pain to see like old Cole did with his bus routes?

Without further thought, Brent got up and walked over to the old-fashioned radiator – a form of heating that the hospital on its limited budget still could not afford to change. He felt its heat, saw its knobbly, scarred surface. Then he went back, got his journal and pen and moved over to a nearby table.

Placing both hands on the white-hot radiator he felt the instant, all-consuming pain but he kept them on the surface until they stuck to the metal as the flesh seared.

Brent Fitzroy was rescued by the ever vigilant Gerald Paxton and rushed to hospital with severe burns to his hands. After months of intensive treatment and skin grafting he was returned to St Clouds where he was able to dictate more immediately realized material into his journal. He no longer had a block. Old man Cole had been sent to him by the gods.

Thoth foresaw the destruction of Atlantis and found his power weakening while the Crystal Pyramid began to sink into the earth. Desperate to preserve and contain Atlantean magical power he designed the pyramid of Giza – his gateway into the physical world, into the third dimension. Thoth then selected Hermes and Aphrodite to supervise the construction.

The Great Pyramid was built in limestone to keep it from eroding and to house the secrets of man since the beginning of time before the last geophysical shift. Its calendar is implanted within the measurements of the steps leading to the so-called King's Chamber. The frequencies of the planets are built into the stone and tempered with crystalline devices that can communicate with the galaxies.

The passageways between the two chambers record the ages of man upon earth and predict the total number of years remaining before the next revolution of the earth's axis.

The pyramids are part of a cradle of a universal grid of ancient religions, political and oracular sites linked to monuments of other star systems.

The pyramid's focal point is placed in the middle of the earth as a living model of mankind's destiny to a higher evolution.

The secret codes of Atlantis are protected by the winged Disc of the Brotherhood of Light. The child is father to the man – the man is father to the child – and so the reincarnations continue throughout the centuries. But the Atlanteans must leave. Their work on earth is finished. I trust Hermes and Isis to ensure their departure.

'All right, old son? Glad to see you working on your journal again. Keeps you busy, doesn't it?' said Paxton one afternoon.

'Busy enough,' replied Brent mildly.

[11]

1

DESTRUCTION AGAIN

Belfast, November 1989

The bomb exploded as Hugo and Jaime were driving down the Falls Road. The dull thud was followed by a dust cloud that hung in the gathering darkness. Traffic skidded to a halt and alarms sounded up and down the grey afternoon street with its boarded-up shops and loitering children. There had been no official warning but Hugo's informant had told him that Declan's was to be the target.

Pedestrians either flung themselves to the pavement or burst into a stumbling run. The blast blew out the bar window and with the shattered glass came the headless body of a man. There was the stench of shit and beer and burning.

They clambered out of the Suzuki and began shooting film, their cameras clicking hungrily at the ravaged exterior of Declan's Bar and the mutilated thing on the ground. Further along the smashed concrete of the pavement, someone ran.

A long period of silence was broken only by the sound of their camera shutters. Then a young boy emerged from the bar, walking hesitantly, a beret pulled down over his head from which a rusty river was pouring, splashing on his scuffed trainers. He looked down in surprise, curiously detached, as if he could not think where the stuff was coming from. Hugo took a shot of the gathering horror in his face while Jaime concentrated on the crimson lake that was flowing into a pile of dog-shit. Then the boy fell, rolled, twitched – and the blood started dribbling out of his mouth as well. He looked up at Hugo and tried to say something, but only made a bubbling sound.

The wail of the rescue services was louder as Hugo stepped amongst the smoking debris. Scattered human remains were everywhere, smudged against the fallen roof, a torso embedded in a wall, a hand under his foot.

The barman seemed unscathed and was leaning against the rubble-strewn bar as if he was ready to serve the next customer, but Hugo ignored him as he focused his camera, taking shot after shot of the charnel house. As the smoke cleared, a small fire shot tongues of flame under a pool table on which lay a body, its fluids seeping into the green cloth; the barman still watched expression-lessly as Hugo shot the grisly image with relentless, clinical application, as if he was a surgeon in some satanic operating theatre. Like Jaime he was a perfectionist who had been at the top of his profession for a long time. That was why they hunted in a pair. Their photographs of destruction appeared all over the international press and their images of violence had been ele-vated to a position far beyond photojournalism.

'How did scum like you get in?' asked the paramedic. There was contempt on the man's face but it had no effect on Hugo; he was used to it.

'Lucky strike. We were driving past.'

'Bollocks.'

Jaime joined them, running off more film while other para-medics, firemen, a couple of policemen and a military sergeant in a flak jacket also filed in; those new to the job looked revolted at the slaughterhouse while others, who had seen it all before, were merely cynical.

'Fucking media,' said the sergeant. 'Piss off.'

Hugo and Jaime ignored him, running off more film as the paramedics gently led the barman away.

Hugo lay on his hotel bed, the twelve-year-old Glenlivet at his side. It was just a few minutes to six and he was thinking of Lucy and Brent in Cornwall, seeing their faces clearly now although he had hardly thought about them in weeks. Belfast was no different from South Africa or San Salvador, much the same as Afghanistan. He was paid considerable sums for his pictures and because he was the best – and needed to maintain the position – his life mainly consisted of airports and bloodshed. There was nothing he would not do to get a good shot; nobody he would not bribe. As long as he was leading the pack, Hugo felt safe; if he was not, an abyss would open up in front of him.

In the abyss he saw inexplicable visions that had recently begun to convince him he was having DTs. Either that or he was on the edge of some kind of breakdown. That was why he was anxious to keep so busy: partly to assuage his guilt for the neglect of his family, but mainly to stop having waking dreams that he could not understand. They had begun two years ago and were increasing, relentlessly assailing him every time he tried to switch off. What was more, Hugo remembered them in minute detail: a great space, a bronze gate springing shut behind him, priests and winged serpents, underground rooms with murals depicting men and women harnessing the energy of the sun, becoming free of self-indulgence, of the cumbersome restrictions of their own bodies, moving towards a chamber where a secret was hidden – and then up towards a rooftop portal through which came a vast sunbeam. The fragments rarely followed one another in any recognizable sequence, and were never all together in one vision; he almost wished they were. Sometimes they occurred when he was asleep, but most often when he tried unsuccessfully to relax. He saw flashes on the television screen, in a dark cupboard, against a wall, through a rain-soaked window – even reflected from a car windscreen. They were momentary – subliminal – but they were there. Sometimes Hugo wondered whether they had any

[15]

connection with his son's obsessive and clearly deranged journal. More often, however, Hugo suspected that he, too, was on the edge of madness and that he and Brent had the same genetic problem.

Jaime was a companion of sorts and sometimes he preferred to drink with him than drink alone and glimpse the inexplicable. Hugo liked to hear Jaime talk of his Catalan home, the small-town life of Toroella where he had grown up, the little art deco cinema, the Sunday mass, the fishing, the trek up the mountain to the hermitage of Santa Caterina.

Hugo's own roots were strictly English middle class: Surrey, the rugby club, university, going freelance, the paparazzi. Lucy. His life had been bright and glossy, competitive and self-congratulatory, loud and frantic – as opposed to Jaime's deep-rooted Mediterranean assurance.

Hugo poured out more Glenlivet and took a long swallow. He had been to Toroella, walked the quiet flagstones of the tree-lined approach to the church, watched the swallows, taken a coffee at the café in the square by the sundial on the flaking plaster wall, seen a movie in the art deco cinema, sat in the Belle Epoque bar downstairs watching the young people of the town protest about military conscription. Here he never saw visions. Toroella was such a stark contrast to his own early life. He tried to remember the person he had been then: a beer-swilling poseur, loaded with confident charm and machismo challenge; sitting in the open-topped Alvis outside the Wheatsheaf Inn with Jack Melis and Andy Graham, going out to bat and returning to the pavilion where the 'cricket ladies' made the sandwiches – halcyon days of hopeful travelling with no thought of a destination, safe in his middle-class enclave, a social success. But even then, particularly then, Hugo had been secretive about his home life, not wishing to have it exposed when he had been at such pains to put it behind him. Now he would like to inter the memories altogether, but that was not yet possible. He could still see his mother doing the rounds of the vodka bottles she had hidden throughout the house, getting less secretive as the long day of drinking wore on. He could still feel his father's absences, see him in his mind's eye caught squirming on the bed with Nancy Sage. Now they were both dead, his mother from cirrhosis, his father from cancer.

[16]

Hugo had been an only child striving to forget a miserable childhood and to invent a new identity. Now it had worn thin again, but not thin enough for even Lucy to know how his parents had been – for he had reinvented them too. He laughed harshly as he refilled his glass. Soon he would feel nothing but the roller-coaster underneath his feet and the protective whisky inside him.

Perhaps it was his parents who had started the madness.

The knock was discreet and he welcomed the intrusion, for he had just seen flickering light on the shadowed wall beside him and was sure that the fragmented illusions were about to torment him again. However many times they appeared he would never become used to them. There had to be a medical reason – one that was connected to the damage he was doing to himself.

'Jaime?'

'Room Service. Message from Reuter's, sir.'

'Ah.' Rather muzzily wondering why they had not faxed or phoned him, Hugo rose shakily to his feet and opened the door.

The sallow-faced young boy dressed as a bell-hop reminded him fleetingly of the teenager staggering out of the shattered bar.

'I'm sorry to interrupt you, sir.'

'That's all right.' Hugo wore jeans over which his paunch bulged, an out-of-vogue grandad shirt which, with his glasses and bullish head, gave the impression of academia going flabby rather than the macho photographer. But his redeeming grace was an air of distinction, grey, intelligent eyes and the rather too carefully groomed head of long, silvery hair.

The boy passed him a folded note. 'Shall I wait for an answer, sir?'

Hugo smoothed out the rumpled paper impatiently. It read: 'If you shout out – I'll blow you away, English cunt.'

Hugo looked up slowly, with a sense of unreality. This happened to the victims in his camera lens. Not to him.

'Who are you?'

'None of your fucking business.'

Hugo had been in difficult situations before and his immediate reaction was to keep talking despite the spreading shock waves, but just as he was about to begin negotiating the boy said:

'There's some new guys in charge, Mr Fitzroy. They don't like the way you work.' The silenced automatic in his hand was steady and Hugo knew that nothing he could say was going to stop what was going to happen. Panic surged inside him and he felt the warm urine seeping down his leg.

'If it's a matter of cash – '

'It's not.' There was something final about the look in his assailant's eyes. He held his gun as easily and as professionally as Hugo held his camera.

There were two slight thuds as the bullets hit him in the kneecaps, and he fell back on the bed, screaming as the hot agony flared.

'Tell your friend the same will happen to him if he sticks around.'

The pain was excruciating; Hugo writhed on the eiderdown as the boy walked towards the door. He did not look back. As Hugo lay there, he saw a woman and a man walking towards him across the deep pile carpet – except that they appeared to be walking on sand. They were hand in hand. Behind them was a pyramid with a portal open at the apex. The sun blazed down intensely. Then Hugo saw Brent, his face radiant, strong, intent, above all sane, running fast across his vision towards the couple. They embraced. His son repeated over and over again, 'We *must* let them go.'

The sky grew purple and dark clouds raced towards him, tumbling down to envelop and soothe away the searing pain. As he was lifted up, Hugo saw the three figures draw apart. The older man was himself.

2

GLIMPSES OF OTHER TIMES
London

Despite huge doses of morphine, the agony lasted for at least two weeks. Hugo had been flown to a private clinic in Harley Street, but it might have been a butcher's shop, he thought resentfully, for all the good it was doing him.

For brief periods, when the drugs had just been administered, the agony was kept at bay, but the pain simply bided its time, a cunning ravening animal, content to know that it would soon be burrowing its way through him again.

Slowly the fire in Hugo's knees dwindled and he became ecstatic, the morphine keeping him on a continuous high. Each word he read, whether in a newspaper or a novel, was of total clarity and vital importance, but he saw no more visions, and neither could he now recall them, except fleetingly, as a dim memory. Lucy sat by his bed every day, her hand in his, cool and soothing, and gradually Hugo recovered.

Dr Lex was small, Scottish, with an Edinburgh accent. His sleek dark hair contrasted sharply with his pallid skin, and as he explained that he was attached to the clinic but had been hired by *Time Magazine* Hugo was conscious of the discreet minty scent of his breath-freshener.

'Do I need you?' he asked politely.

'I'm a psychiatrist, Mr Fitzroy. You've been hallucinating.'

'I've been in terrible pain. I can't remember anything – '

'That's why I put some of what you said on tape.'

'*What*!' Dr Lex stared at him and he added more quietly, 'Why? Why did you do that?' Hugo felt exposed. Had he been talking about the visions? They seemed light years away now.

'Your editor tells me you have been under pressure for a long time. And drinking heavily.'

Hugo said nothing. The drink was such a familiar problem that he no longer felt threatened, just slightly curious.

'Before I play the tape back to you, can I ask you about your family?'

For an appalling moment, Hugo thought that Dr Lex knew all about his parents. Then he realized that it just wasn't possible. He must be talking about Lucy and Brent. 'I have a wife. A son.'

'A son who is mentally ill?' asked Dr Lex.

Hugo stared at him in silence. 'I thought psychiatrists weren't meant to ask questions,' he observed eventually.

'Techniques differ.' Dr Lex's voice was dry. 'I'm trying to establish a reason.'

'What for?'

'Your obsession with Atlantis.'

Hugo gazed at him in astonishment. Could *that* be what he had been seeing in those disturbing fragments that had tormented him for so long?

Dr Lex produced a cassette.

'It's my son Brent who is obsessed with mythological worlds,' he protested.

'Are you concerned about him?'

'Of course.' But in fact he had tried to put Brent out of his mind years ago – just as he had tried to obliterate his parents. He had not entirely succeeded, but if he worked hard enough Hugo could avoid thinking about them for days. And when he could not he drank. Just like his mother had before him. 'He's been diagnosed a schizophrenic.'

'And your wife? What is your relationship with her?'

'We rub along.'

Dr Lex switched on the cassette. 'There will be seven successive renewals on planet earth. Atlantis was the fifth and the sixth has

[20]

already begun with its violent climatic changes and wide-scale natural disasters. The energy is soon to arrive. We will go to the pyramid – Brent and Philippa and I.'

Lex switched off. 'Do you know anyone called Philippa?'

'No.' Hugo did not. His taped voice was flat, neutral, hardly recognizable as his own. It was as if he was reading words from an all too familiar text. The monotone chilled him, and he realized that he was afraid of the darkness his son had already entered. Philippa – he had not the slightest curiosity about her; she was probably only part of a delirium that he must, at all costs, avoid.

Lex switched the cassette on again. 'Unknown to Thoth, the Brotherhood of the Winged Disc was formed to protect the Atlanteans. But only we can enter the Chamber of Records to discover the time of the earth's change in frequency and give them the release they have been denied.'

Again Lex stopped the tape and leaned back in the grey plastic chair by Hugo's bedside. He crossed his legs, smoothing out the creases in his trousers and displaying highly polished black shoes that gleamed in the patch of hard winter sunshine coming through the window.

'Bad dreams,' muttered Hugo. 'That's all they are.'

'What is your interest in Atlantis?'

Hugo watched the dust swirling in the beam of light that still radiantly lit Dr Lex's shoes. 'I don't have one,' he said finally.

'Would you say your drinking was out of control, Mr Fitzroy?'

'You think my drinking's the reason for that babble? DTs?'

'Thoth? Winged Disc? Frequencies? It's all rather specific.'

There was a long silence during which Hugo could just pick up the sound of a television in the open ward next door.

'Do you know why you became alcohol dependent, Mr Fitzroy?'

'I just got desensitized. One job after another in violent places.' It seemed the obvious, acceptable explanation.

Another silence was allowed to develop but Hugo made no attempt to break it.

'Tell me about your son,' asked Dr Lex eventually.

Hugo felt relieved. By going through the motions on Brent it was as if he was taking back control. 'As a child he was introverted – didn't make friends easily. Got locked into fantasy and science-

[21]

fiction and stayed there. He just didn't develop. When he was in his early twenties he started seeing visions, said he heard voices. It was a terrible shock and our GP sent him to a number of specialists. Appointment after appointment – went on for months. In the end he was diagnosed schizophrenic. He's been in and out of St Clouds ever since, permanently obsessed with this Atlantis theme. I suppose he's been in my subconscious more than I realized.' Hugo could see that Dr Lex knew he was being glib and struggled to sound more convincing, but he was suddenly gripped by the feeling that he was alone in a situation he did not understand, that had nothing to do with being shot – but everything to do with the jagged interior life that he had been glimpsing. The room was now unbearably hot and he felt slightly sick, as if he had a fever. It must be the drugs, he thought, again trying to tidy the threat away.

'What about the Winged Disc and the Chamber of Records? What part do they play in your son's illness?'

'I can't remember,' he forced himself to say. 'I once glanced at some crazy journal he kept. Perhaps they were in there.' The fear was mounting and Hugo's stomach began to churn. He fumbled for a handkerchief.

'Tell me about your wife.' Dr Lex switched subjects again and Hugo had the impression that he had noticed his alarm.

'I met her when I was photographing a tin mine. She's a Tregellin – Cornish landowners. All very Daphne du Maurier.' He could hear himself speaking brightly and foolishly. 'Her parents were alive then and they lived in this old manor house called Lizards, perched up on the cliffs. Lucy was training to be a conservation officer. All this was years ago now.'

'Do you spend much time at home, Mr Fitzroy?'

'No. Lucy and I have drifted apart.' Hugo paused, trying to be more objective. 'I suppose I chose to be away. All I really cared about was fulfilling the latest assignment and setting up the next. It became very mechanical, though; wherever I end up, the carnage is the same – just the landscapes differ.'

'Didn't you ever want to go home?' Dr Lex uncrossed his legs and aligned his shiny toecaps with a square in the lino. He was a neat man. The sun had gone and the room was cold.

[22]

Hugo began to speak a little faster. 'I felt trapped in Cornwall. I had to be working, keeping up, being a jump ahead. The drink was a comfort,' he admitted, surprised to find a sense of relief in being partially honest. That was as far as he was prepared to go, though; they were getting too near his real self, the one he had been so successfully hiding from, the person who had run away and was still running, but pursued by – by what?

'Have you ever thought of getting off your roller-coaster?'

'What would I do?'

'Be with your family while you convalesce. Do something about your way of life,' said Dr Lex gently, but before Hugo could reply he added, 'Spend time with your son.'

It was late afternoon and Hugo was alone, lying in bed, looking up at the ceiling, trying to think about the future. He knew that he must see Brent and understand the mental link between them – if there was one. There must be; in some way he was sharing his son's insanity. The idea terrified him, but for once he was determined not to push it out of his mind. He had almost erased Brent's childhood, because he had run out on him and his guilt was enormous. It had lain deep in his subconscious, buried, a submerged monster which could only be doused by alcohol. Now the alcohol was no longer available Hugo felt the pain increasing in him every day – far sharper and much more comprehensive than the bullets that had shattered his knees.

Hugo shut his eyes. He could only see Brent as a child – at his most vulnerable. He opened them again, but instead of the scarred ceiling saw clouds swirling and darting across the face of a hard cruel orb of a sun. Below the bed was the floor of a desert with dunes rolling towards an endless horizon. A wind was stirring the sand and there was a distant thundering that was becoming louder and louder. He seemed to be travelling, yet Hugo could still feel the bed beneath him, rock solid, as an object on the horizon gradually became clearer. Mesmerized, he stared at it, until eventually he realized it was the pyramid. Below him was a woman running over the dunes, looking up at him, her face twisted with despair and anger. 'You're going to be too late,' she

[23]

cried as he hurtled on, the wind rising in ferocity. He could hardly see anything now for the red haze of storming sand, until the pyramid towered above him and he could make out Brent standing in its shadow. He was holding up a book. Like the woman, his features were contorted with angry despair. Hugo did not know what to do. Then, rather like the snapping of an elastic band, the vision vanished with a sound like a gunshot.

Lucy sat on Hugo's bed, her lilac dress crumpled, her face lined. Now that he was looking at her properly he realized she was much thinner than when he had last seen her, and the self-protective look he was only just beginning to get used to seemed more pronounced. Once she had said, 'I'm not going to let you hurt me any more.' That had been a long time ago. Was he only just beginning to recognize a perceptible change?

'I've seen the shrink,' he explained.

'Yes?' There was curiosity in her voice, but it was not strong. Overall she gave the impression of a woman who had given up hope a long time ago.

'He thinks I should come home.'

'Do you want to?'

'Yes,' said Hugo. He spoke self-consciously, as if he expected the affirmation to be welcomed, but Lucy answered pragmatically.

'You have to realize I've got used to you not being around.' She sounded flat rather than uncaring.

Hugo felt a surge of self-loathing. 'I want to try – to make something of our lives,' he said, and immediately sensed her scepticism. He knew how hard it would be. He would have to regenerate himself, cut out the booze, face the guilt and acquire self-knowledge. The kind of psychiatric recipe he had been fending off for most of his adult life.

Hugo lay back, exhausted. Somewhere deep inside, he knew that she didn't want him back, that it was all too late, for their relationship at least, but he was not prepared to let the thought deter him. He couldn't afford to.

Lucy took his hand. He knew she was making an effort, and he could feel the same pain as he knew was locked inside her.

'I don't want to go back to drinking,' he said. She nodded as she always nodded, in a downbeat, unaccepting sort of way. Hugo almost sympathized with her for he knew how many times he had tried to make this promise.

'That's going to be hard.' She released her grip and the pain in his knees seemed to get worse. 'You'll need professional help.'

'I need *your* help.' Hugo thought he sounded plaintive, and despised himself.

'I'll be as supportive as I can.' But she still sounded flat and she fiddled aimlessly with her handbag.

'I don't understand why I quoted from Brent's journal.' She did not reply and he rushed on, the admission bursting out, almost taking him by surprise. 'And I'm seeing things – that don't belong to me.'

'It's because you love him – and you're on morphine, Hugo. It's the drugs that are doing it.'

He shook his head. 'I've been having – these dreams – or whatever they are – for a long time.' He looked at her sharply, wondering if she wanted to know, if she was going to risk getting this close to him again. 'Have you heard the tapes?'

'Yes.'

'What was your reaction?' He sought eye contact.

'I was curious.'

'The extraordinary thing is that I only saw the journal for a short while, and that was years ago. How could I possibly have remembered such large chunks?'

'What he wrote must have made a deeper impression than you thought.' She paused. 'And you were so concerned about Brent that the words got locked away in some corner of your mind – and were released with the pain.' The statement sounded contrived.

'You *will* help me?'

'Yes. But I don't know if you can change, if you won't get out your camera and catch a plane, just from force of habit.'

He had the unsettling thought that maybe she hoped he would.

Over the next few weeks of receding pain, Hugo gave consider-able thought to Brent's journal and the mystery of the visions.

Until now, he had always dismissed the Atlantean obsession as part of his son's condition and he saw no reason to think any differently now. It was all illness – his own as well.

Hugo accepted the offer of more sessions with Dr Lex, but at the same time unproductively resisted the psychiatrist's attempts to draw him out. Although he was genuinely concerned about his drinking, he knew that if he let Dr Lex get too close he would be exposed, and exposure was something he had always feared – now more than at any time. He could still see his mother taking a bottle of vodka from the music stool, and his father riding the warm flesh of yet another whore. Now there were other causes for despair: a wife who no longer needed him and a neglected son, broken, mad and without a future. Hugo felt increasingly at the mercy of his mind and was afraid that in addition to all his past and present miseries, the enigmatic visions would return to torment him still further.

'Atlantis,' said Hugo to Dr Lex at their next session. 'Why Atlantis?'

'Perhaps the theme of Atlantis is a bonding with your son; a shared memory but one that's so deep-rooted you can't remember anything about it,' he replied. There was a long silence. 'Did you tell Brent stories when he was a child?' he asked eventually.

'I wasn't much good at that sort of thing, 'said Hugo.

'Your wife's department?' His voice was expressionless, factual, trying not to spread the ripple of guilt.

'Yes.'

'Was Brent ever trying to tell *you* stories?'

'There was something – but I can hardly remember.' Hugo was cautious, wondering if it was safe to make an admission.

'Try.' Dr Lex sounded encouraging for the first time.

'Once – when he was about six – I remember him standing in the bathroom, looking into a long mirror while I was dressing. He said, "I've seen you before, Daddy," and I replied, "Well – you see me every day," and *he* said, "We were together, weren't we, Daddy? Not with Mummy. Just us. Just us and the other lady." Of

[26]

course I asked him where we were meant to be and he said, "In the pyramid, of course." I just laughed – at the time. Later on I asked him who "the other lady" was, but he wasn't giving any more away. Not after I'd laughed at him.'

'Any other references?' He was still encouraging.

'Not till later.'

'That was the first.'

'As far as I remember.'

'When did you lose touch with him?' asked Dr Lex.

'We lost touch when he went to Marlborough. What did J.M. Barrie say? Something like "there's no life after twelve"?'

'That depends on whether we have abandoned our childhoods or not,' he murmured. There was a slight regret in his voice.

Hugo paused, wondering how much more he could admit. He felt a surge of panic. 'It was wonderful when he was a child. I was working on a local paper and freelancing for the *Sunday Times*. It was the end of the 'sixties and I actually used to believe my work was fun.'

'Did you have fun with Brent?' But he was not in any way condemning.

Slightly nonplussed, Hugo continued. 'We had a dinghy and we used to sail around the Cornish coast. It wasn't a soft touch,' he added defensively. 'The tides are treacherous and the seas heavy. But I knew what I was doing; we all knew what we were doing. There was a small island called Tiderace we used to land on and we made it our own.' He paused, seeing the place in his mind's eye for the first time in years. 'Just a lump of rock, really, with birds and windswept foliage, but it was a paradise to us. We sailed and swam and built fires and beachcombed. Very difficult to land on – even for the locals – but we managed quite well after a few spills.'

'I don't get a very clear picture of Lucy in all this,' interrupted Lex. 'She seems hazy – half formed.'

Hugo felt under attack again. 'She was – is – a fine person, far more generous and willing than I am. She's honest – likes to look everything in the face. Is that less hazy?'

Dr Lex said nothing. He blinked slightly and waited for Hugo to continue.

[27]

'The idyll was unbroken until I reached Barrie's deadline. Perhaps it was *we* who grew up – Lucy and I,' he said sadly.

'Did you really grow up?'

'You mean I'm immature, that I deserted them – '

Again, Dr Lex didn't reply.

'When I got my first assignment for *Time Magazine* one summer, Tiderace didn't happen. And then another summer went by.'

'Did you have regrets?'

'I didn't think – I was too caught up. I remember Brent writing to me that second year,' he admitted. 'I can recall every word of his letter.

' "We went out to Tiderace," ' he recited uneasily, ' "but it wasn't the same. I couldn't find the pyramid. I've been reading about Atlantis though. Love, Brent." It worried me a lot – always has – but I didn't take it seriously enough or do anything much about it. I suppose I was afraid that he was becoming a fantasist, thought he was too much alone and becoming dangerously introspective but wouldn't allow myself to think about it more profoundly. I told him to make friends. Sent him to Marlborough. I mean – he was bright enough. And then he went on to Oxford.'

'What were the first obvious signs of his illness?' Again the gentle encouragement.

'Lucy noticed most of them. But I do remember coming home when Brent was about to go up for his last year. He was still a loner, never had any friends home for the vac, *still* spent God knows how much time on Tiderace. Anyway, we were having a cup of tea in the kitchen and he – Brent asked me if I believed in space portals.' Hugo was much more in his stride now, with the focus on his son rather than himself. 'I said I didn't understand and then he began to explain something about going into a pyramid in Egypt, and meeting a priest who was harnessing the energy of the sun. Brent said that he needed to ask them to forgive him – but he wouldn't tell me who they were. I have to say his manner carried total conviction and he was talking quite naturally, as if he'd been on a field trip. He wasn't intense or feverish and he made his crazy statements seem almost normal, rational.' Hugo dredged more from his memory, surprised at his own recall. He had not thought about all this in years. Then he wondered if he had thought about it at all. 'He said he'd travelled down to a secret room where the walls were painted with pictures that somehow showed the regeneration of the mind. I can hear his voice now. "There is to be a change in the earth's frequency and the opening of a portal." I just stared at him; couldn't think of a word to say. I discussed what he'd said with Lucy and she told me he'd been speaking like this for a long time. We both came to the conclusion Brent needed help fast. Then I went off on an assignment – and Lucy spoke to our GP. It was downhill all the way after that – for all of us.'

Dr Lex nodded. A sunbeam was pouring through the half open window and motes of dust danced in its rays. For a moment, Hugo thought he saw Brent's image reflected in its translucence, and knew that he must still be feverish. It would take some time, he thought hopefully, but with rest and treatment – surely he would get back to his normal self. Whatever that was.

3

ISLAND VISIONS
Cornwall

Brent Fitzroy leant back in his chair in the day-room and closed his eyes. Hetty Kingham asked, 'Is it difficult to remember?'

'No.' His voice was thin and sometimes hard to hear – not exactly a whisper, more like a sound in another room: just audible but not entirely meant for her. But for who, she wondered. Over the last few days, ever since Brent had so deliberately burnt his hands, he had dictated to her.

Hetty was pleased because the job kept her in practice for the higher forms of dictation she had spent her life receiving – from God, the Virgin Mary, the disciples, and, in particular, St Paul. But she also received transmissions from more lowly figures such as Dr Crippen, and Gilles de Rais, Hitler, Mussolini and Goebbels. Should her dictation be interrupted, Hetty would react violently and, recently, when a nurse had brought her milky and over-sugared tea during a session with the Venus de Milo, Hetty had driven the plastic cup up the woman's backside, causing consider-able anal damage. In fact she was a very disturbed and unpredict-able patient who had been in St Clouds for over twenty years. If busily occupied she was stable, but without clients her instability often condemned her to padded isolation.

Hetty was always content for her contacts to take their time, but as Brent was her first live client for many years she did not quite know how long she would have to wait. She sat patiently enough, though, her polka dot dress hitched to the thigh and her shorthand pad placed on a plump ivory knee.

'Are you ready?' asked Brent.

Hetty nodded demurely.

But he still did not begin, and closed his eyes again. To counter her slight impatience, Hetty discreetly glanced at the slightly built young man. Well – he *was* good looking with his shock of washed-out fair hair and long pallid face. He had been more animated when he first arrived on the unit and would enthral her with tales of classical myth, pyramids and priests, space portals and galactic beams, changing earth frequencies and reincarnation. Nick-named by the staff 'the new age prophet', Brent enthusiastically poured out his obsession, talking for hours on end, until most patients went out of their way to avoid him.

But Hetty remained faithful, never bored, always eager to hear more. Brent excited her sexually as well as mentally, and she thought about his body as much as his visions. Over the last year, however, he had become much more withdrawn and had lost a considerable amount of weight. Hetty had noticed sadly that he hardly ever spoke about the pyramid, and would only write in his journal, but now he needed her again. Because of his hands. They were encased in clear plastic and she could see the spoilt flesh. Hetty felt a trickle of perspiration on her forehead and more under her dress.

Without warning, Brent began to dictate. 'The pyramid, a survivor of the Great Flood, was placed at the centre of the earth as a living model of man's destiny to a higher evolution.' He spoke at great speed and without expression. 'Once man can centre his solar and magnetic energy and align this energy with the pyramid, he can be synthesised into new forms of light to go beyond our solar system to other star systems in the universe.' He paused and closed his eyes, as if willing himself to see more. 'They're blocking,' he muttered.

'You can't see?'

'Not clearly. Someone's standing in the way. I can't see the light. It's my fault. I should have managed to preserve Atlantis – when I was Thoth.'

[31]

'Who's there?' A wave of fear swept through Hetty, for Brent looked murderous and there was a dribble of saliva coming from the corner of his mouth. 'Who's there?' she repeated.

'I think it's my father.' He paused. 'Someone's with him.'

'Who?'

'A woman.'

'Your mother?'

'No. Someone else.'

'Here comes the tea trolley,' said Hetty irritably.

'Fuck the tea trolley,' said Brent.

The nurse approached them warily, knowing that neither liked to be disturbed at their tasks, fully appreciative of their capacity for violence. The notebook fell on to the dingy lino as Hetty tried to ward off the encroaching trolley and the nurse picked it up with a quick apology. Not much hope of reading that back, she thought. It was just a continuous flow of straight lines.

'I want to ask you something,' said Hugo as Lucy drove them to the hospital. He shifted his position painfully and uncomfortably in the back of the car.

'What is it?'

'During my absences, was there anyone else?'

She did not reply immediately. 'I need time, Hugo. So do you. Don't let's rush anything.'

'So you won't give me a straight answer.'

'There isn't one.'

Hugo tried to suppress his resentment. She was certainly making it as difficult as possible, he thought angrily.

'I wouldn't rack your conscience too much; Brent would have been ill anyway – whether you were here or not.' She sounded as if she had started out wanting to be comforting but her bitterness had got in the way. What was more, Hugo sensed that Lucy meant the opposite of what she had just said.

'Let's take him to Tiderace,' he said on impulse.

Again she did not reply.

'Lucy – '

'That's absurd.' She was angry, contemptuous, now.

[32]

'They all say, never go back. But suppose we did?'

'Brent can't go in a boat.'

'Why on earth not?'

'He's seriously ill.' She spoke slowly, as if to an idiot.

'Why don't we give it a try?' Hugo persisted.

'Hugo – this is just – '

'Why don't we give it a try?' he repeated.

'Because St Clouds would never agree.'

The male nurse touched Brent gently on the shoulder. He was lying on his bed in a spacious room. The french windows opened on to a verdant lawn, and although there was a motorway in the distance the sound of traffic could hardly be heard.

'Your parents are here.' He didn't move.

Lucy had told Hugo that Brent had gone downhill. Nevertheless, Hugo was not prepared for what he saw, and had considerable difficulty in not gasping aloud with a mixture of revulsion and shock.

Brent's pallor, the scratches on his face, his burnt hands, his whole wasted appearance made him look like a victim. Something's sucking him dry, was Hugo's first thought. Or was it someone?

Brent stared up at him blankly, his mouth, eyes and nose encrusted with slime. Hugo glanced across at Lucy but she seemed completely unmoved. She's used to all this, he thought. But why the hell doesn't she insist they clean him up? How could they leave him in a state like this?

'Could I be alone with him?' asked Hugo. 'Just to give me a chance of getting through.'

'Of course,' said Lucy, briskly co-operative. She looked exhausted. 'I'll go and get a cup of the particularly brutal tea they serve in the lounge.'

With equal tact, the male nurse departed with her.

'I'm sorry I've been away so long.' Hugo reached out for his son's wrist, finding the skin cold and greasy to the touch. A smell of sweat seemed to pervade Brent's body. He did not stir, lying there on his back like a sick child, his cloudy eyes on the stuccoed ceiling.

'I've been having dreams – dreams like yours. Or should I call them visions? They seem to tie up with your journal.'

'Burnt hands.' The voice was indistinct.

'How did that happen?' Of course he knew.

'Burnt them.'

'Yes.'

'Couldn't remember.'

'Couldn't remember what?'

'I don't know.'

'Was it important?'

'It's a life. A life, isn't it?'

Hugo did not understand what he meant but at least they were talking. Somehow he had to keep it going just in case he got lucky. Professionally he was so persuasive. Yet here it was different. He felt threatened.

'Whose life?'

'Lots of them.'

'Are they good?'

'They're hard.'

'Why are you writing your journal?'

'For Thoth.'

'Thoth. Who's he when he's at home?'

'He's me.'

'I see.' Of course his son was insane. There could be no logic – but there might be clues. 'Do you think about me?'

'Who?' Brent's voice was slightly slurred now and his eyes kept closing. What kind of medication was he on? Or was he trying to shut him out?

'Your father. Hugo. Me.'

'Hermes.'

'Who?'

Brent yawned. 'Tired.'

'Been writing?'

'Dictating.' Strangely the word was unslurred, but it sounded like a careless comment uttered by a weary businessman.

'Will you come to Tiderace with me?'

'Bucket and spade, Dad. Let's hold back the sea.' He was still articulate.

'You bet.' Hugo at last felt encouraged, although he did not have the faintest idea why.

The hospital gave permission for Hugo to take his son to Tiderace. Lucy was visibly shocked and tried to demur, but they were both told that Brent had reached such a low state that a carefully supervised and structured trip back to an old childhood haunt might do him some good, or at least, they implied, it couldn't do any harm.

Their decision, Hugo later noticed, seemed to further embitter Lucy, and although she was attentive to his physical needs, the battery of pills he still took and his unsteady walk, she seemed as far apart from him as when he had been away. But there was one relief: he had not hallucinated for days now and had not seen Dr Lex for a week. He did not intend to see him again; Hugo felt that he was off the hook.

The expedition to Tiderace took place a week later. Hugo hired a small but sturdy motor cruiser and Lucy unenthusiastically agreed to accompany them. Brent arrived, docile, seemingly uninvolved, wearing a track suit that was too large and an anorak that was too small. He was accompanied by Paxton, whose jarring cheerfulness irritated everyone.

The morning was blustery with a brilliant blue sky flecked with racing clouds, and the *Dolphin* thumped flatly through the wave crests with Hugo at the wheel, heading towards the island which was about four miles offshore.

Brent sat out on deck in a white canvas chair, watched over anxiously by Paxton who genially made observations about sea and sky which obviously annoyed him intensely. Lucy brewed coffee in the cabin and served it with difficulty in the swell, returning immediately to prepare lunch.

She's happy to withdraw, Hugo thought, not just from Brent

[35]

and Paxton but me as well. What am I going to do if she won't have me back, he wondered with a sudden attack of panic. It was the first time that he had allowed himself to seriously consider life without Lucy. He had loved her, still loved her; or was he in love with the permanence and security of her, the fact that he had assumed she would always be waiting for him? Right now, she seemed remarkably impermanent.

Hugo glanced up at the reddish, sinewy rock. They were approaching the island now and the bright sunlight picked out its rugged shores in silvery detail. He stared at Tiderace curiously, knowing what love and happiness and innocence and self-contain- ment it had held for them, but not really remembering its physical features, so multi-layered had he become.

He looked across at Brent and felt a pang of grief. As he watched him, his son swung round and his gaze met his father's. Hugo flinched as the pale blue eyes locked into his. He turned away, feeling almost as afraid of Brent as he had been of the young intruder in his hotel bedroom. Then, to his intense amazement, Hugo saw the pyramid.

His head reeling, Hugo turned back to his son, and was immedi- ately aware that he was watching the cliffs too. They stared at it in silence, only the low throbbing of the engine breaking the stillness, but as they approached the coast the pyramid suddenly disappeared.

They rowed into the cove in the tender, Brent sitting bolt upright, a bizarre figure but not without a strange dignity. Tiderace looked smaller than ever, bare rock, jagged cliffs, a tiny summit and an undulating path to a plateau full of scrubby foliage. The sea had quietened a little but still pounded at the rocks, sending spray flying up in great spumes.

'Magnificent,' said Paxton, looking robust but chilled as some of the spray came aboard the tender, but Brent did not seem to

[36]

notice anything now, hardly moving as the boat struck the gravelly beach of the cove. 'Get any seals here?' Paxton sounded over-enthusiastic, but his eyes were on Hugo.

'Yes,' said Lucy.

'This is going to be fun.' He sprang out of the tender.

'It's good of you to come with us like this,' said Hugo awkwardly, still dazed by what he had seen. He felt a surge of despair. He was still hallucinating. Would Brent's presence tell him why? What did they have to share?

Brent Fitzroy stood on the desolate beach, looking down at the pebbles.

'Brent, darling. Do you remember this place?' Lucy asked.

'Yes,' he replied. 'I remember coming here.'

Hugo tentatively put an arm round his son's shoulders.

'Who are you?' asked Brent.

'You know who I am.'

'Are you my father?'

'Of course.'

'You went away.' His voice was not accusing, merely matter of fact. Paxton was looking at them all possessively now. Perhaps he'll write us up for a thesis, thought Hugo.

'I had to earn a living – for all of us.' He tried to speak as gently as possible, but immediately the words were out he knew he sounded too assertive.

'Do you fancy a scramble, Brent?' asked Paxton. He sounded slightly threatening. 'Do you remember how we tackled the cliff path at Foy?'

Brent shrugged.

'Are we all going?' Lucy asked grimly.

'I think it would be for the best,' said Hugo. He looked at his watch. Just after three and the sun was intense. 'I've got a couple of bottles of mineral water in the boat.'

The climb to the plateau was comparatively easy, but it was much harder to the cliff top and soon the pain in Hugo's knees was agonizing. Several times he had to stop.

'You shouldn't have attempted this,' said Lucy admonishingly.

[37]

'I've got to.'

'You all right?' bellowed Paxton, who was further up the rock with Brent, one hand protectively on his arm.

Hugo took a grip on himself and tried to shut out the shooting pains. Then Brent called and this time he was animated, almost childlike.

'Race you to the top, Dad.' Brent looked eagerly at his father. There was a light in his eyes and only the ungainly body and institutionalized clothes remained to serve as a reminder that he was a patient. Beside him, Paxton seemed to have suddenly lost his energy.

'Be careful,' advised Lucy but Hugo's knees no longer hurt as Brent grabbed his hand.

'Come on, Dad.'

They climbed on, and as they did so Hugo remembered the times they had shared on Tiderace. In his mind's eye, he saw Lucy and Brent swimming towards him through the breakers, Brent and himself lighting a driftwood fire on the beach, exploring the rock-pools, making castles on the tiny strip of sandy beach, gathering seaweed, skimming flat stones over the waves. They had been happy then – and he had taken it away, a growing future wrecked by the restless need to move on, not to be known intimately, not to be exposed even by his nearest and dearest. Why had he been so afraid? Why had he swopped so much good for numbing sensation-hunting?

Then, as they clambered over the final crest, Hugo saw the pyramid again, gaunt against the afternoon sun, and he cried out, shielding his eyes at the reality of it. This time there was no light, a cloudy darkness around its base, but his feet hardly seemed to touch the ground as Brent dragged him on.

'Dad – can we camp on the island for a fortnight? The three of us.'

'That's what we used to do.' Hugo was panting slightly as they stood side by side.

'It's great, isn't it?'

'How did this get here?' Hugo still couldn't believe what he saw, but when he touched the light grey stone, it felt real enough. He looked up at the walls, seeing hieroglyphs, carvings of animals, and a huge central G. 'What does that stand for?' he asked, as if he was inquiring about a butterfly or a moth that the youthful Brent was showing him.

'Giza.' His voice seemed distant. 'The Great Pyramid, a survivor of the Flood, placed at the centre of the earth.'

Hugo was terribly afraid now; the walls seemed to cast a longer, darker and colder shadow – the shadow of madness.

'The space portal is going to open soon, Dad. The frequency of the earth – it's changing.'

'I don't understand what you're talking about. What's going on?'

Aertex shirts and corduroy shorts. Socks and sandals. So brown, and with a shrimping net. That had been his son. Who was this figure beside him? In a too-small anorak. With a boy's voice.

'You will.'

The pyramid shimmered with an incredibly bright light, and then dissolved back into dark rock.

Brent began to walk towards the edge of the cliffs. 'I've got to be punished,' he said. 'I thought they would welcome me. But they know I'm Thoth, know that I let it be destroyed.'

'Wait!'

He did not reply and Hugo could only hear the sighing of the wind that was mounting again. Brent was very near the edge now, looking down at the boiling sea, but Hugo stood there inert, powerless to help.

Paxton came from nowhere, grabbing Brent round the waist, hauling him back quickly and efficiently.

'We've had our outing,' he snapped. 'Let's go home.' They left Hugo standing on the rock, inadequate and afraid. He began to shake.

*

'What happened?' asked Lucy as they scrambled slowly down to the cove. Paxton was well ahead of them, shepherding his charge back to the tender.

'I saw a pyramid.'

'Don't give me that,' she said dismissively and Hugo cringed inwardly. That's how she used to talk about my ambitions, years ago, he thought, remembering the anger he had felt when she unfailingly dusted his plans down so sensibly, putting each one in its logical place. Change had always been anathema to her, and she subtly resisted anything innovative, or even mildly different.

'Don't you believe me?'

Lucy didn't reply.

'Or would you prefer the theory of mutual hypnosis?' He barked an angry laugh at her as he almost lost his footing on the steep path. Below, Paxton was helping Brent who stumbled on like an old man, hardly able to place one foot in front of the other.

The voyage back to the mainland was silent, the powerful motor boat ploughing through a long swell. Brent was below, asleep on a bunk, while Paxton, openly disapproving, played patience. Lucy sat in the cockpit beside Hugo at the helm. They had not spoken since leaving Tiderace and he felt an increasing emptiness between them.

'It was solid,' he muttered. 'Absolutely solid.'

'Don't let's go into all that again. Can't you see what a disaster this trip has been? If it hadn't been for Paxton – '

'Dr Hibbs thought it was a good idea.' Hugo felt like a child caught out in a lie. He should just have admitted hallucinating. But there had been more. Much more.

'Dr Hibbs was wrong. I want him back in the hospital – safe and sound,' Lucy said distantly. 'And you must get some rest, too – you've overstretched yourself,' she added perfunctorily, and Hugo knew that what she really wanted to do was to take Brent home, make him a cup of cocoa, put him to bed, slip in a hot-water bottle and cocoon him in sheets and blankets, securing him with an eiderdown. But Hugo knew that even if she could, when she had put out the light and closed the door, their son would open the window of his mind and see pyramids and portals. But where was all this leading?

Hugo no longer felt afraid as he steered the *Dolphin* back towards port, and as he looked up at the stars and planets so sharply etched in the clear night sky the words from the tape came back into his mind. 'We will go to the pyramid – Brent and Philippa and I.' Who was Philippa?

Desultory weeks passed while Hugo's kneecaps finally healed. He spent most of his time walking on the cliff paths thinking about what had happened on Tiderace, trying to impose order and meaning – and failing. Lucy had resumed work and went every day to her office in Falmouth. Without her, the rambling house was arid and he had never been a gardener. Contact with fellow journalists was painful for he felt an old crock, out of the swim, unable to talk about anything else but sickness and rehabilitation. Strangely, Hugo began to feel a strong sense of frustration at the loss of his hallucinations. Originally he had been pleased, thinking he was 'cured', but since his experiences on the island he felt a yearning for some kind of corroboration.

When she came home Lucy clearly tried to be sensitive to his depression, driving him out for meals with old friends he could hardly remember and had nothing in common with, or with new acquaintances that he could not be bothered to get to know. They were all worlds apart from him; Hugo had lived on his wits too long, been in too many tight spots, had too many drinking companions to have any patience with their ordered lives. Giving these new acquaintances no chance to be interesting, he held the floor, becoming the grand old man of anecdote, boring himself as much as them. He saw their frozen smiles and their growing impatience, but he continued to punish them for what he considered was their complacency as much as for their obvious antipathy.

In his role as a semi-invalid he had not touched alcohol since his hospitalization, but he simulated drinking with endless cups of coffee, tea and fruit juices. The painkillers had seemed to dull the desire for alcohol, and the several courses of antibiotics he had had for infections of his shattered knees did much the same, but as he healed the desire to drink grew until Hugo found himself thinking about alcohol all the time, making the excuse that perhaps with the return of intoxication he would be able to approach the mystery of the pyramid.

He tried to exhaust himself by walking as much as possible, slumping down afterwards in front of the television, only to find that the ever persistent Lucy had landed him with the Masons for drinks, the Beresfords for a barbecue or Tim and Margaret Jackson for supper. That was the danger point – when he needed a drink the most – so he swopped the buzz of alcohol for the dubious lift of self-invention as his anecdotes became more and more bizarre. Lucy had obviously decided that to criticize Hugo would not be politic and maintained a slightly martyred silence, making them both hyperconscious of the problem.

Occasionally they went out together on their own, but somehow it only extended their nurse/patient relationship and Hugo soon found these times very hard to bear. Neither discussed the ill-fated trip to Tiderace, and Hugo made no further attempt to tell her about the pyramid.

They both visited Brent each week. Hugo took care never to go alone for Brent had deteriorated badly and Hugo knew that the hospital put this down to the visit to Tiderace. Their son seemed to have withdrawn even further into some deep place inside and no longer concerned himself with his journal at all. Hetty now waited in vain for dictation while Brent sat alone in the day-room, his partially healed hands hanging at his sides, his head on his chest and his feet crumpled underneath him. Occasionally he would look up and several times he nodded at his parents or drank a cup of tea held in a shaking hand. But there was no more than that, and although his drugs were changed several times he remained much the same. It was if the very essence of him had been drained away.

'Another wasted visit this afternoon,' said Hugo, as they walked across the sands in the glow of the late evening sun. The sky was dark amber, and the golden line of the tide was beginning to cover the flat, grey expanse.

'Yes?' Her voice was neutral.

'He just *sits* there.'

'He had a bad shock.'

'Is that what the doctors say?' Hugo knew that Lucy had spoken to them yesterday but she had only passed on the barest of details.

'They think he'll only start his journal again when he feels safe.'

'Are you sure?'

'Sure about what?'

'The doctors are such gurus.'

Lucy clambered over one of the breakwaters and Hugo followed, surprised to find that his knees coped easily with the awkward manoeuvre.

'You think we should ask for a second opinion?'

'I didn't say that.'

'Then what do you think?' There was an edge to her voice now.

'Why *did* he try to kill himself?'

'I don't know. He's ill. He's mad.' For the first time Lucy had stopped being careful and her voice shook with emotion. 'Hugo – I can't make it all right for you.'

'Did I ask you to try?'

'We've got to talk.'

'What about?'

'Us.'

The sun had set and there was only a crimson stain left.

'Can't you see I'm trying to make a fresh start?'

She made no response, staring silently out to sea.

'Can't you help me? You said you would.'

'There's something I have to tell you, Hugo.'

He knew what was coming. He could almost see a new uncertainty in the darkening sky. 'What is it?'

'I didn't wait for you.' She half laughed.

'I don't understand.'

'There *is* someone else.'

'Why didn't you tell me before?' he said angrily, furious that his suspicions had been correct.

'I wanted to make sure you were strong enough.'

[43]

'You can't *do* this to me,' he said self-pityingly.

'Believe me – I don't want to.' She was suddenly so much more resolute. It was as if she had hurried across a falling bridge and was talking to him confidently from the other side.

'Who is he?'

'An estate manager. He's called Tim.'

'Is that all you're going to tell me?'

'What else do I *need* to tell you?'

'And what's going to happen?' The last patch of crimson in the sky was swallowed up by darkness.

'I want to be with him.' Hugo could not see Lucy's face clearly and her voice barely reached him through the void. 'His wife is dead. I'd like to live with him. You can have the house.' The staccato sentences had a dreadful finality. 'I'm very sorry, Hugo. I loved you for many years after you abandoned us.'

'I never *abandoned* you – I had a job to do.'

'Left us, then.' She was prepared to modify the terminology. 'When I first met Tim it was just friendship. We were both lonely.'

'Where have I heard this before?' he asked with sarcasm.

'Many times, I would imagine.'

'Can't you reconsider?' He changed tack. 'It's going to be different now.'

'I shan't be moving in with him yet.'

She was right, of course. He had abandoned them. And how could he have been so naïve, or so arrogant, as to have seen Lucy as the conveniently busy conservationist who would remain celibate, dutifully visiting her schizophrenic son, counting the days until her husband returned complete with drinking habit? Without doubt, he had only lived on the surface of his mind, like a dragonfly skating over a scummy pond.

'Do you want a divorce?'

'Not now. I want to see how things work out.'

'There's no chance of us trying again?' He struggled to steady his voice.

'There's Tim – '

'I wasn't suggesting a threesome.'

She shook her head, warding off his feeble attempt at humour. 'I'll be moving out in a couple of weeks.'

[44]

'Don't hang around for me,' said Hugo savagely.

'The last thing I mean to do,' said Lucy wearily, 'is to argue about this. I just want you to appreciate that while you were away, no doubt being outstandingly brave on assignment after assignment, collecting all those awards, not to say the most striking pictures – we were here. Waiting for you.' Her intense bitterness cut through the weariness, chilling him to the bone. 'Finally, you were forced back here – but it was too late. Far too late for me – and Brent. Look what's happened to him.'

'You said his illness would have happened anyway,' said Hugo resentfully.

'He loved you, Hugo. He was close to you, as I was. You gave us an idyll, but only the promise of a future. You never told us the idyll was going to end.'

'I didn't know, either.'

'I *need* Tim. Do you understand?'

Hugo nodded.

'Are you coming back?'

'I'd like to walk on a bit,' he said. 'You go home. No, wait. Will you change your mind?' Hugo asked in sudden desperation. He had never felt so alone.

'No,' she replied gently, the bitter anger temporarily spent. For a split second she hesitated, and then turned hurriedly away.

Left to himself, Hugo walked down to the water's edge, watching the tide gradually coming in with hardly any sound at all. Gazing out to sea, knowing Tiderace was there, he had the unsettling sensation that the past was catching up with the present and governing the future. He had reached a painful impasse. His marriage was over, there was nothing left of the middle life. Was this the old life lapping menacingly at his feet, the expanse of dark water inviting him, drawing him in as Brent had been drawn to the cliff edge? Or could there really be a future? What did his shared visions with Brent *mean*? And who was Philippa?

*

'Do you know who Philippa Neville is?'

Brent, his eyes closed, was slumped in a deck-chair in the gardens of St Clouds. A nurse hovered around a table of other patients and the sun shone out of a glorious May sky that was full of darting, puffy clouds. A stream ran through the bottom of the valley, glinting in the luminous light, its banks studded with cowslips, and a small, pagoda-like bridge linked the grounds to a field of grazing sheep. The idyllic setting, the freshness of it all, contrasted sharply with the pallor of the patients' closed faces and, in some cases, closed-in behaviour patterns, almost as if the sunshine and the pastoral scene was a stage set – a painted world that was mockingly out of reach.

Brent shook his head and Hugo felt a surge of elation at even this minimal piece of communication.

'I think you know her.'

'No.'

'Of her?'

'I'm tired, Father.' At least he was recognizing him today. But Brent was apathetic and Hugo felt a growing, unreasonable, dangerous anger. Could he prise anything out of him with aggression? Were there any short cuts? He was sure that he was notorious with the hospital since the Tiderace débâcle so, in a sense, what did he have to lose; he had lost most things in his life anyway. He also felt physically lonely, as if he had reached a plateau in his recovery and had stopped climbing up – or out.

'I feel we share something. Something important,' he persisted.

'You have to make your journey.' The weary voice replied faintly.

'How do you know I'm going on a journey?'

'I can sense it – like I always did.' The voice was stronger now.

'I'm going on a short photographic assignment.'

'Yes.'

'I'll be back soon.'

Brent did not reply.

'Am I to discover something in the Middle East?'

There was no response and Hugo's frustration grew.

'Look. Do you have anything to tell me?' He was painfully aware of how ludicrous he must seem. Brent was a schizophrenic, incapable of rational communication. What was he trying to prise out of him? Hugo rose to his feet, horrified at what he had been trying to do. 'I've got to go now. I'll see you in a couple of weeks.'

'That's what you always say, Dad.'

'What's that?'

Brent had opened his pale blue eyes and was sitting up, the agitation showing clearly in his face. 'You always said a couple of weeks. But it never was.'

'I'm sorry.'

'You're not sorry. You left me on my own. You're leaving me on my own again.'

'Mum's here. She'll be in tomorrow.'

'You left us both on our own – both of us.'

Hugo knew there was going to be a scene – knew that the situation was running out of control. The sylvan setting seemed to have changed. The sun was behind a cloud, the stream was dark, the flowers and grasses waved uneasily in a scudding breeze, a sheep turned its head towards them almost menacingly. Then the sun came out again, the luminosity returned – but Brent was standing up, holding on to the shaky deck-chair, shouting, 'You've got to be different.'

'Yes.'

'Got to be.'

'Sit down, Brent.'

'Got to be different. You have to start the journey – the real journey – but you won't be able to do it. Not like this. Not as you are. You've got to change.' The staccato sentences were like machine-gun fire. The nurse was running towards them, and out of the corner of his eye Hugo saw Paxton walking hurriedly from the house. Had he been watching them?

Brent collapsed into the deck-chair, a ludicrous Chaplinesque figure, waving hands and legs, an object of mockery and derision – made so by Hugo. Already Paxton was with them, looking grim, lips pursed, talking calmly and quickly to Brent, disentangling him patiently and with dignity.

'We'll have a rest inside,' he said, signalling to the nurse to take his arm. He went, leaning on her, staggering geriatrically, without looking back.

[47]

'I'm sorry.' Hugo felt totally at a loss.

'He seems to react to you badly.' Paxton's voice was neutral, but there was condemnation in his eyes.

'Brent feels I deserted him.'

'He's very ill.'

'Much worse?'

'He doesn't write – or even dictate – his journal.' Paxton seemed to think that was very serious. 'Not now.' He shook his head.

'What does the doctor think?'

'Dr Hibbs feels that he's withdrawing into himself. He's discussing another drug regime with your wife tomorrow.'

'Aren't I to be consulted?'

'I believe you're going away.' Paxton sounded accusing.

'I am.'

Hugo left the hospital feeling that he was escaping again. But what had Brent meant about being different? 'You've got to change,' he had said. 'You have to start the journey – the real journey.' The question was not just what, or even why – but how.

4

THE JOURNEY BEGINS
Iraq

Gus Knowles of *Time Magazine* sat in the back of the beaten-up dust-covered Porsche and yawned. 'How much longer?'

Beside him Hugo checked the camera. The driver, Kuwaiti-born journalist Anwar Hayat, was confident. 'I know the Iraqis are coming over tonight.'

Hugo adjusted his night viewer and tried to relax. Around him the scrub desert landscape rolled into infinity, the sand rippled, soiled with rubbish, ash grey in the moonlight. 'We need you,' the magazine editor had said over the phone. 'It's the big one.' And he had seized the opportunity, unable to think of a reason not to rejoin the old life. There was nothing else.

On the way back from the hospital he had felt guilty and depressed. It had shocked him deeply that Brent had thrown off his silence and withdrawal only to accuse him so vehemently. He had never felt so inadequate. Plunging back into work, he had told himself, was the only way to blot out the ravings of his mad son.

The Kuwaiti shanty town was silent, and above them a huge sickle moon sharpened outlines and penetrated shadows. Hugo heard an argument going on in a one-storey building with a scattering of chickens at its base, a dog began to howl and a radio started up, playing a Muslim singer he had heard before but could not place.

Gus lit a cigarette, got out of the Porsche, stretched and leant against the hood.

'Long time since we worked together. Where was it? Balcombe Street siege?'

'Mmm.' Hugo still felt disorientated.

'How are the knees?'

'They stiffen up, but they're OK. I don't suppose they're ever going to be a hundred per cent.' They talked in half whispers while Anwar read a newspaper by the dashboard light.

'And life at home?'

He paused. This was the first time he had told anyone, but Gus, like Jaime, was an old mate. 'Lucy's left me.'

'I'm sorry.'

'It was coming – but I didn't see it. She's moved in with someone else. Given me the use of Lizards, though. No doubt she's simply bearing my schizophrenic son in mind,' he added bitterly.

'In case he comes home?'

Hugo shrugged.

Two hours later tanks, trucks and armoured cars crossed the border and drove past the shanty town in seemingly endless procession. Hugo, lying in a stinking rubbish-strewn ditch, took shot after shot. A rat ran past him. Somehow its presence seemed appropriate.

The convoy showed no sign of abating. Apart from the drone of the traffic the desert night was still, and he could see that the lights in the shanty town had been doused. But he also knew its inhabitants were gathered at the windows, watching the vehicles, wondering what was going to happen. He remembered Biafra and the Sudan, the Palestinian camps and Somalia. The ordinary people, illiterate and dependent on the land, forced on route marches that would predictably kill their children and later themselves. Eyes full of flies, swollen stomachs, diarrhoea and the deadly cramps of dysentery were all these people had to look forward to.

Hugo joined Anwar who was still in the Porsche and Gus arrived a few seconds later as the procession rumbled on.

'I've never seen anything like this.' Gus was shaken.

'It's the invasion.' Anwar displayed little emotion. 'That bastard Hussein, he'll burn in hell for this.'

But Gus was not so sure. 'Surely he's bluffing.'

'Bluffing?' Hugo was scornful. 'With that convoy? He wants to give Bush a bad time – and by God, he's going to do it.'

They huddled together in the Porsche, the rumbling on the desert road no longer disturbing them. Hugo slept lightly.

The headlights woke them at about four.

'Armoured car,' whispered Anwar.

The vehicle had pulled up a few metres away. Two Iraqi soldiers got out, walked to the door of a small stone-built house and began knocking with the butts of their rifles. Hugo viewed them with professional detachment, as if he was watching a movie. Ever since he had arrived in Iraq he had felt a curious sense of unreality.

No one came to the door so the soldiers began to splinter the pitifully thin wood with their boots. As they did so, more armoured cars rolled into the square until the whole area was lit with blazing yellow light, rather like a film set.

A jeep arrived with an Iraqi army officer in the back and Hugo felt the first dull twinges of alarm. Because the Porsche was parked behind an outbuilding, they had so far remained undiscovered, but with a sinking heart Hugo knew that it could only be a matter of time.

'We've a right to be here,' said Gus defiantly, but Hugo sensed that he was feeling much the same as he was. Rights had not prevented him being knee-capped.

'Where can we get under cover?' he asked.

'There's a school house over there.' Anwar's voice shook.

'What do you think, Gus?'

[51]

'Let's go.'

The Iraqi soldiers were breaking down more doors and a young man was being dragged out. His protests ended in a choke as one of the soldiers clubbed him in the balls with the butt of his rifle. He fell to his knees, clutching at his testicles, emitting little whinnies of pain until one of the soldiers laughingly kicked him in the stomach. The young man instinctively rolled himself into a womb-like position, but his punishment continued.

'Come on,' said Gus. 'For Christ's sake – '

But Anwar didn't move. 'Someone's coming.'

Hugo glanced into the wing mirror, his mouth dry.

'It's a kid.'

'What's he doing?'

'Watching us.'

'Why can't the little bastard sod off?' muttered Gus.

Other residents of the shanty town were being dragged out of their homes now and it was becoming clear that the Iraqis had instructions to evacuate the place. The officer was out of his jeep, supervising the rounding up, barking instructions and pouring coffee out of a thermos. Dogs were barking incessantly and a woman's voice rose in prayer.

'Let's go.' Gus inched one of the Porsche doors open as silently as he could, but despite his caution its dry hinges gave an appalling squeak that seemed to drown the dogs and the shouting.

'What about the kid?'

'Forget him.'

They managed to get the other two doors open without so much noise. A man was sobbing and the officer was beginning to lose his patience.

Hugo and Gus followed Anwar, pounding over the rough ground, so far unnoticed by the soldiers, but when he glanced back, he saw that the boy was following them like a stray. As they ran a shot rang out from the square.

*

[52]

They huddled inside a small concrete building that housed a generator and the boy followed, standing imploringly on the threshold.

Anwar snapped at him in Arabic but he remained there, small, thin and wiry, his eyes dependent. Then he burst into rapid speech.

'What's he saying?' asked Hugo.

'The Iraqis took his uncle – and he's got no one else.'

'We can't help him – ' began Hugo.

Gus, however, was more generous. 'Tell him to come in and shut the door.'

Their visitor was surprisingly helpful as he dived behind the generator and pulled up some rubber matting to expose a hatch. He opened it and disappeared.

'Oil store.' Anwar began to clamber after him.

Hugo followed, and Gus pulled the mat over the hatch as best he could.

It's like being in a grave, thought Hugo. They were crouched together in the oily darkness, bodies touching, and the boy was beside him, rancid with sweat. He closed his eyes and, wedged between the others, wondered if he could sleep and blot out their predicament. But of course the idea was absurd.

They waited together silently, straining their ears, but could hear nothing. Time passed. Conscious of every movement the others made, every contraction, every drawing of breath, Hugo's cramped position became increasingly intolerable. He caught a suppressed fart, a tiny gurgle of gastric juices, a tentative clearing of a throat. He felt the boy beside him, warm, sour, shifting a little from time to time until he longed to hit him. Something crawled across his face and he slapped it away, startling them all and making Gus grunt in protest. Something else, soft and tiny-boned, ran across the dirt floor in front of them, touching his palm, but this time Hugo was able to control his revulsion. Time continued to pass, but he would not look at his watch, knowing that once he kept checking the minutes would crawl by like hours.

[53]

Then he heard a movement above – and the hatch was pulled back so suddenly that they all gave a little whimper of surprise and fear. The torch shone down on them with a hard brilliance, running over their features with detached interest. Dimly, Hugo could see shadowed faces that seemed neither hostile nor friendly.

Then the boy was scrambling over their heads, clutching at the arms above, chattering happily to the soldiers who pulled him up, patting and kissing and praising him.

'What in God's name is going on?' demanded Gus.

'It's his way of earning money,' Anwar replied. 'The little bastard set us up.'

'English?' asked one of the soldiers, crouching over the pit.

'American,' replied Gus. 'Knowles – *Time Magazine*.'

'British. Photographer for *Time*.' Hugo could hardly bring out the words.

'Anwar Hayat. Kuwaiti. Independent Press, working for *Time Magazine*.'

'We didn't know who you were,' said Gus smoothly. 'But now we do – there's no problem.'

'This is war zone. Unauthorized.'

'We didn't know that – '

'Kuwaiti. You come out.' He repeated the instruction in Arabic and Anwar slowly clambered out. 'Over there.'

Hugo could see his feet. Anwar wore expensive slip-on leather shoes, and there was a slight scuff mark on the side of one of them. The shots rang out – maybe four or five – and the shoes skidded forward on their heels. There was a dull thump and Hugo could see Anwar's arm. There was blood running down the wrist in a stream. He watched it hypnotically, too devastated to call out or even speak to Gus, aware there would be no reprieve this time.

'You.'

Gus stared up at the soldier blankly.

'Out.'

The cold sweat poured down Hugo's face. Please, God, no.

[54]

'Listen – ' Gus fought to stay calm.

'Out.'

'You shot my colleague in cold blood. You'll be court-martialed for this. Do you hear me? You'll be fucking executed – ' Gus was losing all control now; his voice rose ludicrously and the boy laughed excitedly.

'Come out.'

'You bastard – '

'Come out, or I shoot you now.'

Hugo could hear the reloading of a pistol.

Slowly, Gus hauled himself up. 'Don't worry,' he said, turning back to Hugo. 'They had Anwar because he was a Kuwaiti – they won't do anything to us.'

'Won't they?' muttered Hugo, shifting so that he could see at least part of the floor above.

Gus stood in front of a young Iraqi soldier who could not be more than twenty. Meanwhile, their informer looked on, grinning, anticipating reward. The sweat poured into Hugo's eyes and Lucy's face swam into his mind. *You* forced me back to this. But he knew that he had forced himself.

'You've got to listen to me.' Gus was pleading now. 'Where is your commanding officer? I *must* speak with him. You are doing terrible things – things without his permission. Do you understand? You will be in very serious trouble. You are – '

The sound of the shots seemed immensely loud and reverberated in Hugo's head for a long time afterwards. The bullets hit Gus in the neck and head and most of his features exploded with the impact. Brain, tissue and other matter mingled with the blood that splashed on to the floor. With his hands making little clutching movements, Gus toppled over.

Hugo began to vomit.

'You come out, English.'

He shook his head.

'Now!'

The boy giggled and there was the flare of a match as one of the soldiers lit a cigarette.

'You come out.'

Hugo curled himself up womb like and began to sob.

'You come out.'

But he only curled himself tighter.

'You come out. Now!'

Hugo shook his head again, and closed his eyes rigidly against the sheer, unbelievable horror of it all. Lizards and the Cornish coastline and Tiderace flashed into his mind only to be replaced by the boy in the hotel with the gun – not that much older than the child who had set them up. Both grinned mockingly at him in his mind's eye and then disappeared into darkness – out of which the pyramid rose on the cliffs of Tiderace, distinct, majestic and beautiful. He had not seen it in weeks, but this time its presence must surely presage death.

He was pulled out of his hideaway and dumped painfully on the dirt floor. Still he did not open his eyes, knowing the bullets were going to tear him apart. Some instinct told him he would soon be able to enter the pyramid. Who was that waving from its shadow? Brent?

'Open your eyes.'

Hugo clenched them tighter shut, smelling shit and sweat and carnage. He touched something soft, jelly-like, and rolled away, gasping in revulsion.

'Open your eyes.'

The cold barrel of the revolver was jammed against his head.

'If you do not open your eyes I will kill you.'

They're going to kill me anyway, thought Hugo. But he opened them as the pressure of barrel against bone increased.

He was lying face downwards, the young officer kneeling beside him, holding the gun to his head.

'Get it over with.'

'I'm not going to kill you.'

Hugo could not believe what his tormentor had just said. He was obviously playing some game.

'I *said* get it over with.'

'And I told you I wasn't going to kill you. Get up. Get up now.'

He took the pistol away but kicked Hugo hard in the side. Numbed by the dull pain he staggered up, catching sight of the corpses of Gus and Anwar. It was hard to imagine they had ever lived they looked so doll-like; even the massive pools of blood seemed artificial.

The officer shrugged and half smiled as if to disassociate himself.

Hugo glanced at the faces of the other soldiers. Most of them were young, perhaps in their late teens. Then he looked down at the child who had led them there and saw that he was still grinning.

In a mist of blind rage Hugo dealt him a stinging blow around the face, followed by another. There would have been many more if the officer had not pistol-whipped him. The boy cried silently, no longer amused or triumphant and Hugo, despite the searing agony in his face and the blood that clouded his vision, felt a passing satisfaction.

The officer turned to the boy, gave him some money and then spoke sharply to him in Arabic. He ran out sobbing.

'You are to be taken to Baghdad.'

'I demand to know why I'm being arrested.' Hugo stuttered out the words, wiping at his bleeding nose. Was it broken, he wondered.

'For having the wrong papers.'

'You haven't even asked to see them.'

'They are wrong.'

Hugo looked down at Gus's body. A tiny burst of wind escaped the corpse. 'You'll be court-martialled,' he said weakly.

The officer smiled and turned impatiently to his companions. 'Take him to one of the trucks.'

'You're illegally invading Kuwait,' yelled Hugo.

'This is our territory,' said the young officer. 'Kuwait is part of Iraq.'

The soldiers took Hugo outside. He did not resist.

*

The truck had no windows, and the journey took a long time. Wedged between two guards, Hugo wet himself and then slept, his comatose state such a blessed relief that each time he was jerked awake he tried to burrow deeper into unconsciousness. The fact that he was back in a situation like this struck Hugo with an extraordinary sense of irony, but the images of the pyramid lingered. 'You have to start the journey.' Brent's voice repeated itself over and over again in the blank cavity of his mind. Was *this* the beginning? Surely he couldn't have meant a journey to Baghdad.

Hugo almost laughed aloud as he realized how wild his mood swings were becoming. Sometimes he put Brent's visions down to madness – at other times to some kind of spiritual directive. But as the truck rattled on he wondered if in fact his journey had been bypassed, and the fatal move had been to take up his career again, to agree to this deadly assignment. Or perhaps it was a baptism of fire, a necessary reminder that he had to make a new beginning to his life. Could he ever stop cutting and running? Fooling himself? Massaging his insecurity with booze and sensation? What had Brent said about change? Being different? Could he regenerate himself? It was odd, but the word stuck in his mind and grew large. Regeneration.

The truck eventually came to a halt and Hugo was half carried, half pushed through a large garage into an austere modern building, across an empty hall and then downstairs into a corridor that smelt of stale excrement and disinfectant. Gradually Hugo became aware that he was passing a number of empty cells until they arrived at the furthest. His escorts had now been joined by an elderly man with glasses who searched him and took away his possessions. The door was then opened and he was pushed into darkness.

Groping around, Hugo discovered a mattress hard up against the wall. There did not seem to be anything else in the small space but a toilet bucket, which stank so badly that he gagged. Numbed by the misery of it all, he slumped down on the filthy mattress, and oblivious even to the bugs once again took refuge in sleep.

When he woke, without his watch, Hugo had no idea how long he had slept except that he felt from his light-headedness and sharp hunger that it must have been for a considerable time.

Looking around him, he realized the cell was now cloaked in muddy light, and a tray of rice had been pushed through an aperture in the door. The tray also contained a plastic mug half full of greasy-looking water, and he ate and drank ravenously, not allowing himself to think of anything but his stomach. Then, slowly, he looked up at the dim ceiling where he could see two vents through which wan light was seeping.

Gradually the light from the vents faded and pitch darkness returned.

An identical tray of rice and water was pushed through the aperture later, but Hugo could not work out how many hours had passed.

This was to be the pattern for what seemed to be many days and interminable nights, and although he tried to judge how time was passing by the repetitive meals Hugo soon lost count. Gradually the numbing shock began to wear off and hot panic swept over him. He shouted loudly and eventually more feebly for guards, supervisors, officers – anyone who would take responsibility for his plight. No one came, and he sank on to his insect-ridden mattress and tried once again to lose himself in sleep. But now even that release had become elusive.

Gradually Hugo realized that he had been brought here to be broken and that the Iraqis had some purpose in doing this. But what could it be? He knew nothing. Slowly he began to wish he had died with Gus and Anwar. The word regeneration came into his mind again and he laughed savagely. What hope did he have of that here?

More days passed – or at least, he supposed they did – and Hugo's desperation grew. No one came to tend to his toilet bucket which now almost overflowing and stank foully. Soon his body odour competed with that of the bucket, but gradually, mercifully, he became less conscious of it and at last began to withdraw into himself. Regeneration no longer seemed absurd.

His mind was an empty space – lofty, enormous, devoid of anything but cathedral-like serenity. Slowly Hugo lost touch with his body completely, seeing the pyramid grow above him until its apex touched the roof, a brilliant light shining from its portal. It was like welcoming back an old and trusted friend. Slowly, comfortingly, he realized that not only was he at home here, but all the protective layers of self-deceit were beginning to slide away. He was becoming whole, for the first time in decades.

The tepid light of dawn was stealing through the vents when the cell door swung open, and in some confusion Hugo imagined that somebody had come to join him inside the pyramid. Instead, he was marched back across the great, bleak hallway of the prison and into a small, windowless interview room, equipped only with a desk and two chairs. Behind the empty desk sat the elderly man with glasses he had seen when he first arrived. Dressed in a light blue suit, his shirt open at the neck, he was now nodding casually at Hugo's filthy, stinking body as if he had arrived at the reception desk of a hotel.

'You will want a shower – and some breakfast.'

Hugo stared at him, too bewildered to respond.

'I'm afraid your confinement was necessary. You were arrested in a security zone. Of course, we immediately contacted your employers, *Time Magazine,* and I have spoken to their lawyers, but I was unable to arrange for you to be visited. Yet.' There was a significant pause. 'You will be released if you can assist us.'

'Assist you?' Hugo tried to take a grasp on reality. 'How can I do that?'

'You were arrested in a security zone,' his interrogator repeated.

'That doesn't give you the right to do what you did. You murdered two of my colleagues.' He was beginning to function again and felt the anger return.

[60]

'Unless you can help us you won't have your shower, Mr Fitzroy. Or your breakfast. We have a number of Kuwaiti prisoners of war here in Baghdad – many high-ranking civil servants, a police chief, a couple of ministers. We want you to photograph them.'

'Smiling happily?'

'We wish to assure the United Nations that we are caring for them.'

'Whereas you've no doubt been keeping them as you kept me – like animals, deprived of light?'

'They are prisoners of war.'

'Why don't you get one of your own stooges to photograph them?'

'Because you have a reputation, Mr Fitzroy. An international reputation.'

There was a long silence.

'No,' said Hugo eventually.

'We also wish you to interview them,' his interrogator continued, as if he had not heard.

'And repeat the lies you put in their mouths?'

'I should like you to reconsider our proposition.' The elderly man was still mildly polite and the eyes behind his spectacles were brown and gentle. 'Take that shower right away. Your breakfast is almost ready.'

Hugo was taken down another corridor and into a modern washroom. There, his guards watched him peel off his filthy clothes and walk into the sheer physical joy of a hot shower.

In the cubicle he found hair and body shampoo as well as cologne and talcum powder, and when he reluctantly emerged his own soiled clothes had been replaced by a shirt, trousers, socks, shoes and silk underwear. He dressed slowly, luxuriating in the feeling of cleanliness, and was then led into a small office where a lavish breakfast had been laid, with a pot of strong coffee and, best of all, a jug of fresh orange juice.

Hugo feasted. Calling for side orders of toast and coffee, he savoured every mouthful. As he ate he tried to think what he

[61]

should do next, but his mind fortunately refused to go beyond his physical well-being.

When he had finished, Hugo was led back to the interview room.

'Did you eat well, Mr Fitzroy?' asked his interrogator. 'And the clothes? They fit?'

'They're fine.'

'So it's good to be civilized again.'

Hugo said nothing.

'And you've decided to help us?'

'No.'

There was a long pause.

'That is a pity.'

Hugo did not reply.

'A very great pity, for it would be – quite terrible for you to become – uncivilized again.'

Hugo still did not reply.

'You will be returned to your cell,' said the elderly man. 'And this time you will be deprived of food.'

'Ray Sipoltski of *Time Magazine* – he won't allow that.'

'We are at war with America, and with her allies. Your Mr Sipoltski is not relevant.'

'Saddam Hussein will be taken prisoner and tried for war crimes – ' Hugo began.

'I don't think so,' was the mild reply. 'We shall starve you for a few days – and then talk to you again.'

'It won't make any difference.'

'I think it will.'

'You are both foolish and ignorant,' said Hugo, too angry to care that the whole exchange was becoming pointlessly childish. 'Even if I did take your photographs, it would be obvious I must have been under duress.'

'I disagree.'

'That's *why* you're both foolish and ignorant.'

The expression of kindly inquiry remained on the elderly man's face. 'Have you anything else to say, Mr Fitzroy?'

'Yes. Iraq illegally invaded Kuwait and murdered my colleagues.

No doubt many others have also been killed. It is only a matter of time before you surrender to the allies and the war-crimes tribunals begin.'

'A speech of true Churchillian grandeur,' observed his interrogator drily.

Back in the cell, darkness became twilight and then brightened again in the now familiar sequence which was the only variation in Hugo's void-like existence. He soon returned to his filthy, soiled state, his new clothes only emphasizing his squalor, but worst of all, once again, the pyramid did not appear. At first he thought he was not concentrating hard enough; then he began to panic.

After a couple more days without food, Hugo started to hallucinate, although he only saw the Cornish cliffs with Lucy walking along them, occasionally Brent and later a terrifying combination of both.

On the third day Hugo was visited by another interrogator, younger this time, and more abrasive.

'You have decided to help us?'

'No.'

The man came nearer.

'You *will* help us, Mr Fitzroy.'

'No.'

He drew back a booted foot and kicked Hugo as hard as he could in the stomach. Then he did it again.

The beatings and starvation continued whilst Hugo slipped in and out of consciousness. One night, however, when he was left alone, he was filled with exultation for now he was on Tiderace, and the pyramid was on the cliff top. He could hear the surf thundering below and a light salt wind played on his cheek. The gate was open and he and Brent walked casually inside.

'Mr Fitzroy.'

The voice was a long way away, hardly penetrating his consciousness.

[63]

'Isn't it great, Dad?' said Brent in his nine-year-old voice. He wore an aertex shirt and khaki shorts and sandals. The pyramid was enormous – so high that he could not see the roof – and there was a cool, dry slightly fragrant atmosphere. A group of priests stood in a beam of light that came from high up in the apex; the shadowed walls were painted with pictures of the human mind, some anatomical, others impressionistic, all filled with luminosity.

'Hugo Fitzroy.' The voice echoed in the pyramid, gentle, almost caressing.

'It's in the journal, Dad,' said Brent distantly.

They joined the priests in the brilliance of the beam and at last the portal opened. Racing clouds were darting across the face of the sun, rhythmically plunging them in and out of the light.

'Mr Fitzroy. Hugo?'

'Who is it?'

'You won't know me, but I'm a friend.'

The vision faded and Hugo opened his eyes to see a tall, dark-haired woman somewhere in her late forties who at first seemed strangely familiar; then the familiarity vanished and he knew he must be talking to a stranger. Her eyes were slate grey and her long narrow face was sunburnt. She had a pronounced air of intelligence and a subtle quality that Hugo found instantly comforting and curiously discerning – as if she already knew him. Screwing up his eyes he tried to bring her into sharper focus but only registered that she was wearing a dressing-gown and her face was bruised.

'Who are you?'

'Philippa Neville,' she replied.

5

HUMAN SHIELD

'You've been out cold for a couple of days,' she was saying. 'They fed you intravenously. I guess they thought you were going to die. They beat me, but not like you.'

'What are you doing here?'

'They wanted me to write propaganda. I told them – no way. Not a chance in hell.'

Where had he heard her name? The answer was somewhere on the edge of his memory. 'Are you a journalist?' he probed cautiously.

'Kind of.' Her smile was tentative.

Hugo gazed round him, his awareness slowly returning. He was in a small, well equipped hospital ward, but despite the constant bustle in the corridor they were alone.

The name. Her name. Where had he heard it before? He searched the burnt-out hollows of his mind and still came up with nothing.

'Do you see a pyramid?'

Now Hugo remembered where he had heard the name before.

'Yes,' he admitted, and was overwhelmed by a profound sense of relief.

The words tumbling over each other, clamouring for release, Hugo told Philippa Neville everything that had happened since the boy had knocked on the door of his hotel bedroom. When he had finished, he lay back exhausted, but exorcised.

'What have you seen?'

'Everything you've talked about.' She spoke slowly, tentatively, but with a quiet authority. 'There's a few gaps. But the pyramid always came back.'

'What does it all mean? I feel we've shared so much already – but how have we done that? How?' Hugo was desperate that the good fortune – the breakthrough – should not suddenly evaporate, peter out into nothing more than half-remembered dreams.

'That's what we have to find out.' She stood up. 'Are you scared?'

'Yes.'

'What of?'

'I don't know,' he admitted. 'Whatever all this means – whatever it *is* – I feel we're meant to be together, all three of us, and we have to go to the pyramid.' But even in his own ears the conjecture sounded childish and incomprehensible.

'Secret mission?' She smiled. 'Across the desert on a camel? Do you see yourself as the Sheikh of Araby? Should I be slung over the saddle?'

They laughed and then looked away as Hugo's anxiety returned. 'Maybe Brent isn't mad after all, but has special knowledge. I don't know how or why,' he finished rather lamely.

But Philippa was impatient with his vagaries. 'We have to work on this, Hugo. I've got this – this certainty that if we *want* to understand the connection the rest will follow. It's all there, but we have to crack the code. But that's what life's about, code-cracking, isn't it? That's the way it's sure been for me. You may have been a cynic, Hugo, but all *my* experiences tell me there's a mystic side. It's just that most folk don't see. But I know it kind of runs parallel to our lives. Like in another room.'

'I don't think we should try too hard.' Hugo sounded positive, as if he *was* slowly convincing himself of a finite truth rather than an ambiguous shadow. 'Now that we're together I'm sure we can do it – if I can peel away the layers of self-deceit.'

'I know what you mean,' she said unexpectedly and for the first time her voice lacked confidence. 'To go back to the people we were before we started inventing ourselves – that could be a downer.'

'I've certainly invented most of myself – sometimes I think mainly for reasons of self-protection – but in doing so I've lost everything. How in God's name do I get back to what I was – whatever I was? You say you invented yourself, too, but I don't see much sign of that.' He laughed, but without any humour.

Immediately Philippa reached out and lifted his hand to her lips. 'We'll go back together,' she said. 'You're not unique, Hugo. We all paper over the cracks – and there sure is plenty of paper over mine. But there's something buried, and that's the link not just between us but with Brent too.'

'I don't think the Iraqis are going to let us do any personal exploration, do you? They'll lock us up again. Separately.'

There was a long silence while they both recognized how powerless they were.

'Tell me about how you became a writer?' He realized that she had told him nothing – that he didn't know her in any way. Hugo cursed himself for his usual arrogance.

'There's not much to say. I majored in Middle Eastern history, wrote a book about Iraq that got good notices in the press. When the Gulf War broke out, I got sent to a news agency in Kuwait to write up an eye-witness report. Then I was arrested.'

'And earlier?'

'My life story will have to wait. You need sleep. I've been in here a week. You haven't.'

Hugo nodded, his exhaustion was like a leaden weight. 'You'll still be here when I wake up?'

'Sure.' She let his wrist go and a wonderful drowsiness came over Hugo as if he was a child again and was being tucked up in bed by a mythical mother.

Hugo slept deeply for another twenty-four hours and when he woke he saw Philippa, reassuringly standing at the bottom of his bed. Her eyes met his and he could feel her relief. It was good to be needed again – even in these extreme circumstances.

'What time is it?'

'Just after 3 p.m.,' she said quickly, but he could see that her original calm had disappeared and she looked drained and tense.

'What's the matter?' he asked, sensing some new and unpleasant development.

'An Iraqi CO showed up this morning. He said we're being shifted.'

'Where to?' Hugo was weak and alarmed, not feeling up to being moved anywhere.

'To an aircraft factory. We're to be part of a human shield.'

'What's that supposed to mean?' he asked, still muzzy from the long, dreamless, visionless sleep.

'The Yanks have been told if they bomb key installations they'll be knocking out hostages. Hostages like us – mainly British and American nationals.'

'You mean they're going to turn us into targets?' Hugo tried to sit up but the weakness would not allow him to do anything so dramatic. 'We've got to talk to the embassy – to *Time Magazine*. They can't do this to us.'

'They can,' replied Philippa.

Just before sunset, some young soldiers arrived in combat fatigues and, ignoring his protests, briskly lifted Hugo on to a stretcher, but his outrage had become grim acceptance of yet another traumatic move. They were given no indication as to where they were being taken, hurrying silently along narrow, unpainted corridors which smelt of disinfectant and defecation. As they passed an open ward Hugo glimpsed the casualties of war sprawled upon mattresses, their bandages soiled with congealed blood. He shuddered, the bile rising in his throat, while Philippa, her face grey in the half light, whispered, 'We're together – and we're going to stay together.'

The aircraft factory looked indecently exposed, with runways snaking out into the desert and uncamouflaged buildings which included two large hangars. The truck pulled up outside one of these, and as the rear doors opened and Hugo was carried out a distinguished-looking middle-aged man in uniform hurried towards them.

'Welcome committee?' murmured Philippa.

'I am Colonel El Him Jala.' He was benign and apologetic. 'I am sorry to meet with you in these circumstances.'

'So are we,' said Hugo. He would have felt less at a disadvantage had he not been lying on the stretcher. 'You realize you won't get away with this. We have both been illegally arrested and subjected to torture – totally against the rules of the Geneva Convention. The war crimes commission will be – ' But his set speech petered out as Colonel El Him Jala held up a hand in mock protest.

'I am sorry, but we are at war. You are both civilians, and you were arrested in areas you should not have been in. But I am not here to debate that with you now. We will try to make you as comfortable as we can.'

'This is way out of line.' Philippa tried half-heartedly to follow up Hugo's tirade. But she knew there was little point in official protest. They were no longer human beings – simply insurance policies that might not hold good.

'You will *have* to accept it. The allies have illegally declared they intend to bomb our installations. We are a small country; we have to take what measures we can against imperialist aggression.'

'Don't you think the invasion of Kuwait was just a touch imperialistic?' asked Philippa, not prepared to give up entirely.

'We are reclaiming territory that is rightfully ours and has been annexed from us,' said the colonel dismissively.

'Bollocks!' said Hugo.

'The allies have had sufficient warning not to bomb these buildings,' he continued placatingly. 'I'm sure you will all have a quiet night.'

'When do we get out of here?' asked Philippa.

'As soon as hostilities cease. When the Americans come to their senses.'

'They're waiting for you to come to yours,' observed Hugo drily.

*

The inside of the hangar smelt of oil, stale tobacco, unwashed bodies – and something less obvious that Hugo instinctively recognized as fear. Lying on mattresses, sprawled on incongruous red office chairs, leaning against dark-streaked walls, sitting on oil drums, were about fifty civilians. The atmosphere held such tension that Hugo could almost touch the raw nerves of the hostages. Judging by their beards they had been here some time, and he could detect from the fear in their eyes that they saw death approaching but did not quite know when it would come. He had seen that look before.

Their arrival only caused minimal interest, but as Hugo's stretcher was placed on the floor a short, stocky man joined them. He had an official air to him.

'Do you understand why you're here?'

'Sure,' said Philippa, 'we get it.'

'I'm Robin Latimer. I was on the British Consul's staff.'

Philippa gave an edited version of their experiences, sounding as smooth and polished as if she was at an embassy reception. Glancing round, Hugo sensed in the hostages the synthetically cheerful yet deadening spirit of 'muddling through'; it was only their eyes that gave them away.

'Can't we form some kind of action committee?' he asked.

'We've tried,' said Latimer. 'But the building's been surrounded and our negotiating potential is, to say the least, strictly limited. We don't know what's happening, what politicians are saying, what our chances are – whether the allies know we're sitting targets and how they'll react if they *do* know.'

'So we're going to sit back and wait for Armageddon?'

'The great escape won't help us,' replied Latimer, with the calm detachment of the vintage British hero.

Who does he think he is, wondered Hugo. An officer in Colditz? 'So what will?'

'We've had various ideas. One was to try and protect ourselves by building some kind of shelter in here. But when we started ripping up the place, the Iraqis stopped us. Another was to try to tunnel out, but the ground's rock solid. So, at the moment, I'm afraid you'll find our imaginations a little infertile.'

[70]

Latimer stayed talking a little longer, but soon he moved apologetically away, muttering that 'they must all get their thinking caps on again' and perhaps they could do with a coffee. Hugo winked at Philippa and got slowly off the stretcher.

'Dashed fine chap,' he told her.

He leant against an oil drum, clasping the plastic beaker, finding the instant brew as comforting as childhood cocoa.

'Tell me more about yourself,' he asked Philippa. 'I don't even know if you're married.'

'No – I don't have anyone.'

'Tell me more.'

She paused, knowing that some at least of her life story might help to keep anxiety at bay. She sought for a starting point. 'You know what we said – about peeling away the layers of the onion. I remembered something weird last night and maybe – maybe it's a lead. I was born in La Jolla – a small town near San Diego. I guess I was a privileged kid; my dad was an attorney, Mom in real estate. I was the love-object, much prized, too much pampered, brought up by nannies. I was lonely. I could have had anything I wanted in the world – except my folks. When I was twelve this Mexican woman showed up. Her name was Elena and we got real close. She believed in reincarnation and at first I was always kidding her but she won me round.'

'How?' Hugo was suddenly alert, aware now that what she was saying was, in some way, of the utmost importance.

'We were walking along the cliffs, down towards the surf. The light was so strong it gave the coast a bleached-out look – almost like a photographic negative. Elena looked down at the beach and said, "That's what you were, Philippa – in your other life. In all your other lives."' She paused and then continued slowly, digging deeply into a past she had swept away. 'I saw this woman striding across the sand. She was naked and I remember giggling. Then I saw that she resembled me – could have been the big sister I knew I didn't have – and I was scared. The woman was hand in hand with a man and he was naked too. It was as if they were both at the beginning of something.'

[71]

'Who was the man?' said Hugo, although he already knew the answer.

'It was you,' she continued slowly, confidently.

'I know it was you. I identified you straight away. We've been together for a long time, Hugo. In other lives with other names.' She waved away his incredulity. 'Last night I dreamt we were watching this pyramid rise up out of the desert. Someone else was with us. Another guy. He was called Thoth.'

'My son.' The shock waves raced through Hugo and he felt an elation he had never experienced before.

Later, he slept, and this time he stood again in the beam of light inside the pyramid. Beside him was Philippa. They both gazed up towards the portal which was opening to reveal a slowly rising sun. Then he heard Brent's voice.

'Dad – '

'Over here.'

'I can't see you.'

He was staggering towards them in his hospital dressing-gown, institutionalized, idiotic, pitiful. In one hand he clasped his journal. Pages were falling out of it, scattering around the floor of the pyramid and then slowly fluttering up towards the light.

'I can't see you.'

Hugo reached out for Brent's hand, and then woke.

It was the early hours of the morning and the atmosphere in the hangar radiated apprehension.

'How's it going?' she asked.

'I feel stronger. Did you sleep?'

'Sure.'

'Did you dream?'

He was about to tell her what he had seen when a voice in the darkness cried out hysterically:

'They're coming!'

[72]

'Try to keep calm,' said Latimer. He reminded Hugo of an ageing Scoutmaster.

Now they could all hear the ominous whine of approaching aircraft – a whine that was becoming slowly, steadily, relentlessly louder until Hugo thought that the allied bombers must be directly overhead. Sirens began to wail.

The hostages were standing silently, straining to hear, and the tension was sharpening, becoming unbearable. Predictably, Latimer began to intone the Lord's Prayer. Hugo took Philippa's hand.

The first explosion shook the hangar. Then came another.

'That was close.' As Latimer spoke, part of the hangar roof began to collapse and Hugo and Philippa made a stumbling dash for some metal worktops a few metres away. As they ran, slabs of concrete began to fall, and choked by black dust they just reached sanctuary as more debris descended. They crouched there in silence, but the remainder of the flat roof held.

Hugo looked around him; men were getting to their feet, hazy in the floating dust.

'Look,' Philippa whispered.

A door had been blown in at the rear of the hangar.

The cold grey dawn of the desert brought them both to a standstill as dunes rolled to infinity below a sullen sky. The thread of a road snaked across the sand, but there was something so primeval and hostile in the dusty, relentless landscape that they stood transfixed.

A black pall of smoke hung over some of the smaller factory buildings and there were craters on the runways. Activity seemed concentrated around the smoke and he could see a couple of jeeps speeding towards the damage.

'I might be able to start that truck over there if we can get in,' said Hugo.

Philippa shrugged in disbelief. He might just as well have suggested commandeering the camel they had laughed about.

[73]

The battered vehicle was parked a few yards away from them, its square body still in shadow.

'I guess that road might get us to the border,' she said reluctantly, 'but we stand a chance of being shot up – on the ground or by an aircraft.'

'So what shall we do? Go back to Latimer and tell him we'll be good hostages and wait for the rest of the roof to fall in? With the truck at least we'll have a chance.'

Hugo walked over to the vehicle and tried the door. Why did he know that it would be open? He clambered inside and found keys in the ignition. 'Christ.'

'What's going on?'

'The keys are here. It's as if we're being offered an escape route.'

'The hell we are.' But she did not sound particularly surprised.

Shadows swept across the desert as the sun edged slowly over the horizon. The truck made a spluttering sound – and died. They exchanged glances, but when Hugo tried again the engine began to turn over.

'The gates are open,' Hugo said uneasily, feeling his strength returning. 'This is too good to be true.'

'Gas?'

'Full tank.' At the back of his mind was the halting knowledge that this was right – that this *should* be happening.

Philippa got in beside him and the high-sided truck rumbled out of the compound.

'Security's lax.'

'They're coping with the bomb damage,' Philippa replied. The vehicle rolled wildly as Hugo negotiated potholes.

'I don't suppose they give a shit how many of their hostages got killed – '

'Or made their escape.'

The truck rumbled out on to a Tarmac road.

'What about water?' asked Hugo.

Philippa scrambled with considerable agility into the rear and then gave a cry of triumph. 'There's a drum right here.'

[74]

Hugo glanced back to the compound and his optimism rose even further as he still saw no sign of pursuit. The keys, the petrol, the open gates, the water – what the hell was going on? It almost looked as if someone had deliberately arranged an easy escape for them. But if so, who did they have to thank? And why?

Gradually the sun rose, turning the sand into a dun-coloured ocean frozen in rolling waves. Apart from the odd derelict vehicle and a few pieces of unidentifiable scrap metal, nothing broke the contours and the road stretched on towards the horizon, undulating slightly but never veering from its straight course.

They drove on without passing another vehicle or seeing a helicopter or an aircraft, the landscape remaining monotonously unchanging.

'We've got about three-quarters of a tank of diesel now,' he said suddenly, tapping at the wavering needle. 'Let's hope the gauge is accurate.'

'It might get us there. I *think* it's about a hundred miles to the Iraqi border.'

'So we could end up walking. The age of miracles may not be with us, after all.'

The road was now running over sand-hills and the horizon was repeatedly lost as they dipped up and down. Then above the rattling and roaring of the truck they heard the chatter of a helicopter.

The truck shook as Hugo squeezed the last drop of speed out of its ill-tuned engine, but soon the aircraft was hovering directly overhead and the sound of its rotors was deafening.

'Piss off,' said Hugo, clenching his teeth, willing the pilot to lose interest. 'Just piss off.'

Forcing himself to lose speed, Hugo tried to look casual, putting an elbow out of the window and appearing as bored as any Iraqi driver crossing all too familiar landscape.

'He's tracking us.'

'Just stay calm.' Hugo was sweating.

'He's coming in.'

Hugo accelerated slightly and then regretted it. The pilot must not think he was panicking. The rotor blades were much louder than the truck's engine now and his head reeled with the metallic tumult.

'For God's sake – ' he began.

'He's going up.'

Slowly the helicopter rose, gained height and flew ahead of them for what seemed like eternity.

'What's going on?' gasped Hugo, trying to wipe the sweat out of his eyes.

The aircraft wheeled and headed for the horizon.

'I'll have to stop,' said Hugo a few minutes later. 'I feel lousy.' His heart was pounding and he felt feverish.

'Keep going.' Philippa was ruthless. 'There's some kind of building up on the horizon.'

Grimly he drove on, seeing the shimmering outline of some-thing insubstantial. He knew he had to get past as normally as possible, but without warning a red haze burnt across his eyes and Hugo only just had time to switch off the engine before he passed out. As his head buzzed with pain and fever, he thought he heard the sound of winged serpents. They were floating in his mind until he saw an open casket. One by one, the creatures went inside.

Philippa was beside him, letting water flow into his mouth. 'We're in the guardhouse of some kind of bunker that's built into a sand-hill,' she was saying. 'There's no one around but the place is all secured.'

Hugo sat up, his head aching. She poured more water into a dirty plastic cup and he sipped at it gratefully. Never had he tasted anything so good. Philippa poured out more and he continued to drink, oblivious of anything else.

'Maybe there's some fuel here. It looks as if the place has been abandoned in a panic. Could mean the allies are getting nearer.'

Hugo glanced around his surroundings. There were a couple of desks, a filing cabinet, dirty coffee cups in a sink, a photograph of Saddam Hussein in full military uniform, a calendar with a highly coloured picture of a mosque, and a fire extinguisher. What does it all mean, he wondered, as he heard again the unmistakable sound of the winged serpents. Were they still in his mind, or not?

When Hugo felt stronger, they walked slowly and cautiously out of the guardhouse, ducked under a security barrier and began to examine the structure of the long, low building that was half buried in the sand-hill. It was just after one and the sun raged fiercely above them, a red blob of suffocating heat.

There were no windows and a steel hatch at the front, but on the side wall there was a metal door that looked as if it had come into contact with the back of a vehicle. Hugo rattled at it but it remained obstinately shut. Then he swung at it with the heavy metal of the extinguisher, and there was a crunching sound as the door shuddered.

'Something's giving.'

Suddenly they were gazing into a dim, cool interior.

'Christ.'

Beautifully painted in acrylic, standing majestically against a setting desert sun, was the pyramid.

'We're meant to be here,' Philippa said when she had recovered from the shock. 'That's why it was all OK. The truck – the helicopter flying away – '

Hugo stared at the picture in silence, afraid for the first time since they had left the hangar. But this kind of fear was very different. It was deep inside him, familiar but not realized for a long time. It was atavistic.

'Let's go,' said Philippa.

Somehow he forced himself to follow her.

*

They walked slowly and apprehensively down a dim, cold corridor, gradually becoming conscious of a sharp, chemical smell. Philippa pushed open a set of rubber doors to reveal an empty room. The floor was covered in blue linoleum and across it was a trail of glutinous, metallic-smelling liquid which in the darkened space seemed to have a slightly luminous glow. The trail led to another set of rubber doors. They found themselves in a small, oblong room whose walls were covered with computer screens and terminals. Facing them were a series of keyboards. There was a sterile neatness, a slight hum from the equipment and more of the metallic liquid on the floor.

'What the hell *is* all this?' Hugo's mouth was so dry he could hardly speak. Was she as afraid? He glanced at Philippa and was amazed to see her so calm. 'Is this some kind of missile base?' he asked, perversely determined to find a rational explanation to dispel his increasing anxiety. 'But there's no launching site.'

'Maybe that's someplace else,' she replied.

Hugo sat down and shakily began to run his hands over one of the keyboards.

Without warning the pyramid appeared on every screen. Mechanically, as if in a trance, Hugo depressed more keys, but the image remained, shimmering slightly. Then the pyramid disappeared, to be replaced by a muddy-looking interior, dark and shapeless. The fear churned inside him again, but the screen was so dim that neither of them could make anything out. Then a number of globes floated across from one side to the other.

'There's a winged serpent in there – or it sure as hell looks like one,' whispered Philippa, but almost immediately the globes began to disappear and the screen went dark. Hugo continued to play with the keys and the pyramid briefly returned, shimmered and then vanished.

'I heard them,' he said slowly. 'I heard them – just before I passed out.'

*

'We've got to get going.' Hugo gazed at her unseeingly, his head splitting, his mind scrambled. He had trouble making any decisions at all let alone putting them into words. 'If they see the truck from the air, it'll look much more suspicious parked here than moving.'

'We need diesel.'

They spent another ten minutes searching the remainder of the building but there was no fuel – only a canteen, kitchen and dormitory, all of which seemed to have been abandoned quickly for the beds were unmade and there were dirty cups and plates in one of the dishwashers.

'It's three o'clock.' Hugo stood outside the white brick building in the searing heat. He was full of foreboding. 'Let's go. There's nothing else here. If we've got to walk then at least we can do it at night.'

'Are you scared?' she asked.

'Shit scared. I think we're being led into something that doesn't have anything to do with us as we are now – but as we were. Perhaps we could have coped with all this much better then. What do you think?'

'Like you.'

He saw she was grinning at him and some of the tension eased. This was the beginning of the journey Brent had been talking about. He was certain.

The sand-hills were behind them now, flat desert rippling away on either side. There were no clouds in the huge afternoon sky and the sun was intensifying. Occasionally they passed a mimosa tree whose roots were reputed to be vigorous enough to find water. Their frond-like branches trailed to the ground, offering a little shelter, but Hugo was driven on by an overriding sense of urgency. He did not want to stop now, however exhausted he was.

'I still don't understand this lack of traffic,' he said eventually, very conscious of the relentless descent of the petrol gauge.

'I'm sure it's the allied advance. The Iran–Iraq war hasn't been over for long – so there would have been zilch communication anyway.' She spoke distantly, as though her preoccupations were elsewhere.

But as if to support Philippa's theory they began to pass the remnants of battle: shot-up tanks half buried in the sand, jeeps, buses, armoured cars, mostly burnt out, lying at the side of the road. There were also a few anti-aircraft guns – or what was left of them – and dozens of skeletal trucks.

They drove on, the sun sinking lower until it plunged into the sand, leaving an eerie, jaundiced twilight.

'It's getting darker,' said Hugo.

'And colder.'

'How many miles?'

'Ten?' she hazarded.

A bird flapped its way across their path and then hung listlessly in the air above them.

'Vulture?' Hugo tried the ghost of a laugh.

'I think it's some kind of crow.'

Still the truck rolled on, with the needle hovering on zero and occasionally dipping below. Then the engine spluttered and died.

'That's it.' Hugo clambered out of his seat and disappeared into the back of the truck. A few minutes later he re-emerged with two gourds which he had filled from the water container. 'These were on the floor.'

'Neat.' Philippa shivered and Hugo put his arm round her. 'What's getting to us?' she asked, but he knew she did not expect a reply.

They climbed down on to the shadowy road, immediately feeling lost in the wilderness. Above them the stars seemed much more starkly bright than usual and a sickle moon, looking as if it was made of aluminium, was turning the sand to a livid white.

They walked away from the truck in silence, and soon Hugo was conscious of being on a treadmill that led nowhere, for the desert landscape was still completely unchanging, monotonously sterile.

'We should get some sleep,' Philippa said at last.

'The temperature's going down much faster than that fucking fuel gauge. We'll stop soon. Get a couple of hours sleep – and then keep walking. Should make the border by dawn.' He tried to sound optimistic but it was not easy. His knees felt unbearably stiff and he was becoming increasingly worried about the road. Suppose they weren't on the border road at all? Suppose it just petered out into the nothingness of the desert? Was that the reason there was no traffic? Could Philippa have been wrong? The Tarmac seemed to narrow slightly and a cold night breeze spread little flurries of sand over the battered, heat-blistered surface.

'Suppose this isn't the road to the border?' he asked truculently.

'Of course it is,' she said briskly, sounding like a nanny.

'Could we have missed the way? This could just be a service route to the base from some other installation.'

'You're talking crap,' she said angrily, the motherly briskness gone. 'We both need sleep. Let's take a break in half an hour.'

Of course, that was it: he needed sleep. Everything would be better in the morning. That was what he used to tell Brent when he was a child. 'Don't worry – it'll all be OK when the sun comes up.' He half laughed at the pretence; another part of him needed it.

They crested a small hill and stopped; in the pale moonlight they could see quite clearly that the road had petered out into the sand.

'You weren't talking crap,' said Philippa unwillingly.

They huddled together for warmth, trying to blot out the disaster and fortify themselves against the coming day. Gradually the cold increased and Hugo was unable to relax, his mind racing. Then he realized what they had to do next. The thought was inescapable and had to be enacted.

'Make love to me.'

He had never found sex so good. With Philippa it was a totally different experience from his guilty couplings with Lucy and the frantic grapplings with whores in faraway places. And there was a further dimension – the halting suspicion that they had been

[81]

together before, that it was not all a dream. And sure enough, as the orgasm came, memory stirred and he was certain they had made love before.

They held each other tight against the cold, and despite their isolation and the fear of what was to come, Hugo had never felt so joyfully liberated, although he also knew that they could both die in a few hours.

'Do you recall?' she asked gently.

'There are shadows somewhere in the back of my memory, but they don't make the kind of sense I want them to.'

'They won't leave us to die out here,' she said confidently, sensing his anxiety. 'Look what happened yesterday: we were protected, taken on a journey, shown the task, and then dumped out here, but to make love, to regenerate other.'

That word again, he thought. Another part of the puzzle falling into place. Who *are* they, wondered Hugo with foreboding. Philippa sounded far more positive than he, but then she had not been conditioned to be a sceptic as he had. Whatever was stirring inside him now had been implanted at a much earlier stage of her life. She had not pursued such a successful course of evasion, and as a result she accepted much more immediately that the mystical life had grown within her and that they jointly had a mission to fulfil.

'Have you thought that our guide might also be our enemy?' he said, deliberately playing the devil's advocate.

'Maybe. But we've got each other. That's what we've always had.' Her confidence irritated him.

'Does that give you such blind faith in our strength?'

'Not blind. We aren't being taken to the pyramid to lay back. They sure as hell need us for something big – something they can't take on.'

'Something we could die for?'

'Perhaps. Are you ready to die, Hugo?' She laughed, but without humour.

'If I had the sure and certain knowledge that we'll be together again in some other life.' But he could see from her expression that she knew he lied.

'Did you *ever* believe in reincarnation?' she asked him.

[82]

'I never gave it a thought, but then I was wrapped in so many layers of self-delusion. The more I shed them, the more I feel renewal – like the earth after a long, hard winter.'

'Are you scared?'

'Very,' he admitted, and then added quickly, 'but I still don't feel I know you. You've told me so little.'

'While you've told me so much? Well, less has happened to me than you – maybe because I've been in preparation. That's why I can believe more easily than you can.'

'I wish to God I'd met you earlier.'

'We were meant to meet now – for this frequency change – whatever that is. Can you credit this? All the way through school and university I never made too many relationships, and even those were at the most detached level. It was as if I was marking time. Waiting.'

'Better than destroying people.' Hugo's voice was savage. 'That's been my forte.'

'At least you've been close to them,' she said sadly.

'Before I destroyed them?'

'I didn't say that.'

'But that's what happened.'

Sensing his pain Philippa hurried on. 'There's another aspect to all this. It's something precious that kept me from going down when I couldn't reach anyone. I felt – something inside. Like a foetus that never developed.'

Hugo gazed at her. There was an expression in her eyes that he did not understand and he felt a surge of anxiety. He ran his hands nervously over her stomach, but found only the tightness of hard muscle.

'So far I've accepted the impossible – which gradually got to be the possible,' he said slowly. 'Why shouldn't there be worlds within worlds? Reincarnation? Winged serpents? Pyramids with portals? But this – this is something else.'

'Do you think I'm fooling myself?' said Philippa defensively. 'I even went for a scan.'

'And?'

'There was nothing there. I expected that.'

'Yet – '

'I still feel the presence.'

'You said it was like a foetus.'

'Sure.'

'Are we talking in the abstract?' he said in sudden exasperation.

'I don't know. And there's – there's something screwy about my right eye. Well – ' she corrected herself, 'not screwy, exactly. I noticed it a few months ago.'

Hugo drew her to him and in the grey light of the slow desert dawn saw a winged serpent, quite distinct and in the centre of her pupil. Within seconds it had disappeared.

'You saw it.'

'Why didn't you tell me before?'

'I don't know. Perhaps I hoped it wasn't there.'

'And you're afraid?'

'Sometimes. But there's comfort too.'

'What are you frightened of?'

'The end of the journey.'

They lay together, holding hands, watching the steely dawn creep up on the desert, its surface becoming saturated with deeper colour as time passed. Slowly the sun rose.

'What's that?' asked Hugo, pointing to a dark shape shadowing the sand.

'Looks like some kind of disc,' she said.

They gazed up into the empty sky.

'You're shaking. You still cold?' She held Hugo tight.

'I'm thinking about that winged serpent in your eye,' he replied. But he was not just thinking – he was consumed with a primitive jealousy, the force of which he had never felt before.

6

THE WINGED DISC

'It's coming back.'

The dark shape appeared again on the desert floor but there was still nothing above. The appalling thought still possessed Hugo: that she belonged to them – that she was already part of them. He grabbed her arm but her flesh was hard and cold.

'Philippa!'

She didn't reply.

The shadow flew lower, and in its density he saw buildings consumed by a vast wave. In a cacophony of sound, Hugo heard Brent's voice, young and fresh but guilty, contrite, owning up:

'I want to make amends, Dad.'

'How?' Hugo whispered, clinging to this last tenuous thread of familiarity.

'You've got to find the time the frequency changes. You've got to let the Atlanteans go.'

'Why *are* they in the pyramid?'

'They're in hiding. The few that are left. You can find the time of the frequency change in the Chamber of Records. You've got to be quick.'

'Why don't the Atlanteans know?'

'The pyramid was built under your supervision. Only the reincarnates have the knowledge. Don't forget, Dad; the child is father to the man.'

'And Philippa? Why does she have a winged serpent in her eye?'

'Because she's a part of them. She needs to be – so we can square the circle.'

That was exactly what Hugo had been afraid of.

The disc shadow began to rise and Brent's voice grew fainter.

'What must we do next?' implored Hugo.

He could not hear the reply, muffled in the stillness, as if a curtain had suddenly been drawn between them.

Hugo stared into Philippa's eyes but he could not see anything now. The fact that he could not, however, did not reassure him. The reverse, in fact. It was inside her, waiting for release. For birth. He was certain. And he was afraid.

Exhausted, they slept again and Hugo saw himself standing in front of the pyramid with Philippa and Brent by his side. Above the apex floated a globe. He could see oceans and land masses but the land masses were changing, taking on new forms as he watched. A door in the side of the pyramid opened and they went inside, their steps making no sound, the silence absolute except for a gusting wind.

They walked into the all-penetrating beam, basking in its mellow warmth. Hugo took Brent's hand and then Philippa's, but the heat became intense, searing . . .

They both woke to a burning midday sun. Moving to the shade of a mimosa tree, Hugo and Philippa slept yet again, but this time without visions.

The sun was setting when Hugo woke with a stinging headache and a throat so parched he could hardly speak. Philippa was standing up against the skyline, the last rays of sun casting great patches of emerald light on the desert floor.

He moistened his lips with water and then took a couple of precious sips. 'We ought to get going,' he said quietly, and seeing

[86]

her anxious face put his arms round her and drew her close. 'I promise you we'll stay together, that I'll never desert you,' he said gently, but Philippa shook her head.

'You can't promise any such thing,' she said bleakly, but Hugo felt an unexpected surge of hope. What was it Brent had said about changing – being different? Well, he was changing. He'd accepted the journey, and now he was shouldering the problem of Philippa.

Half an hour later, as they crested more sand-hills in the strong, sharp moonlight, they saw the road emerging again from the sand. Somehow this seemed as plausible as the visions.

The headlights began as indistinguishable dots and then grew larger, like shooting stars. There was no cover at all and neither Hugo nor Philippa made any attempt to conceal themselves.

A few minutes later, a battered jeep skidded to a halt beside them, and the driver leapt out. Short and powerfully built, with long, black hair, he was wearing a dirty white shirt and jeans and holding a flask in his hand.

'Mr Fitzroy?' There was considerable authority in his voice. 'Miss Neville?'

They nodded.

'My name is Tarik Ibrahim. You were observed by an Iranian reconnaissance helicopter. I've come to see if you would like to take a ride?' He smiled and offered them the flask. 'Or were you just taking a promenade?'

'The road vanished – and then showed up again,' said Philippa. 'We had a long hike.'

'It was blown up last year and the desert moves in fast. You were fortunate you took the old road. The new one is swarming with military traffic.'

Hugo could see a rifle casually thrown across the back seat of the jeep and tried to gather his senses. 'How do you know who we are?' His voice was hostile.

'Security.'

'Whose?'

'Iran. You have nothing to fear from me, Mr Fitzroy.'

[87]

But Hugo knew they had everything to fear. The desert interlude was over.

'I was told you managed to escape from the Iraqis and were heading for the border – at least, that's the direction you were making for when the chopper saw your truck.' Ibrahim gazed at them. It was difficult to interpret his attitude. Hugo saw it as a cross between patronage and curiosity.

'Have you identification?' Philippa was as wary as he was.

Ibrahim pulled out a battered leather wallet. Inside was a card printed in Arabic and in spite of everything Hugo had to repress a smile. It could have said anything: FISHMONGER; DENTIST; REFRIGERATION SALESMAN.

'I realise you have no reason to trust me.' Ibrahim shrugged, implying that he did not particularly care either way. 'But at least we can talk. You'll be interested to know I was educated at Harrow, and then Oxford. I'm a civilized Arab. Quite one of the chaps.' He spoke with such assurance that Hugo decided to take a calculated risk. He wanted to challenge him, to surprise him into revealing who he was really working for.

'We found some kind of monitoring station out there,' he said, and Philippa frowned, clearly apprehensive, knowing he had made a serious blunder.

'What is it, then?' Ibrahim's response seemed elaborately casual, but Hugo could see that he was now suspicious and cursed himself for being such a fool.

'Neither of us are in any state to talk now,' Philippa put in quickly. 'Are you going to get us out of this god-damned desert or not?'

'I'm taking you to a hospital.'

'What about the border?' demanded Hugo uneasily. 'We don't have any papers.'

'Don't worry. As long as you're with me, there won't be any problems.'

They clambered stiffly and painfully into the jeep and Ibrahim drove them away. Hugo sat listlessly beside Philippa. There was total silence between them; she seemed to have become a stranger again, clearly condemning him for flying a kite that had crashed.

The border post was twenty minutes away – a hut, a security gate, the flag of Iran and a jagged fence of barbed wire. After a few words from Ibrahim a guard waved them through and the jeep roared on into the desert night, its headlights blazing like the eyes of a hunting animal. Hugo shivered, the atmosphere of hostility threatening to engulf him.

'I'm taking you to a private military clinic.' Ibrahim's voice broke into his misery. 'It's on the edge of the desert and no one will ask you any questions – other than those about your health. You'll find the facilities excellent.'

'And then?'

'After a short debriefing, we shall be making arrangements to repatriate you,' he said surprisingly. 'Once at the clinic I shall leave you in the safe hands of Dr Rashid. When he decides you are sufficiently recovered I shall come and talk with you again.'

Was that a threat, Hugo wondered, but made no comment. Now they had returned to civilization, the winged serpents and the pyramid seemed distant but he still felt deeply oppressed as he remembered the winged serpent in Philippa's pupil and heard again his own voice stupidly arousing Ibrahim's suspicions.

Hugo and Philippa were given adjoining rooms in the Pahac clinic managed by the benign Dr Rashid. He was young, but although he spoke to them gently, with reassuring warmth, Hugo remained sceptical. They were here for a reason – and it had nothing to do with their health.

The clinic resembled a five-star hotel with luxuriously appointed rooms and fittings, gourmet Middle Eastern food and discreet, attentive service. Hugo, however, had poignant memories of the well-equipped shower and clean clothes of the Iraqi prison. Was all this simply part of a softening-up process? There seemed to be no sign of it immediately, however, and when Dr

Rashid suggested they ring their respective editors they were amazed to discover the Iranian authorities had already been in touch with them. But instead of relief, Hugo felt only as if someone had called half-time.

'We're going to sell a lot of copies,' his editor told him over a crackling line. 'You've scored, Hugo – more than you've ever scored before. Congratulations.'

'I've no pictures,' he replied dampeningly.

'Who wants pictures? You've got the story, haven't you?'

Philippa's editor reacted with a similar cynical ecstasy.

'If the Iranians have gone as far as making this kind of contact, then surely they'll let us go back,' Philippa said to Hugo, needing his reassurance but not getting it.

'I don't trust them. And I want to know more about that monitoring station – or whatever it was.'

'They'll never wear that. We must just accept, be open to whatever happens. This isn't an assignment – or an investigation.' For the second time she was angry and remote and Hugo realized that he was still hanging on to the threads of logic – the idea of some kind of 'story'. Philippa's consciousness, on the other hand, was firmly rooted in another world. Why couldn't he accept that? Surely he had enough evidence? Or was he still uncommitted, still half suspecting that the visions were the stuff of madness? Grimly Hugo knew that he must hang on to what was left of the rational – which wasn't much. Someone had to be on their guard.

'I want to find out who Ibrahim really is.'

'Stop trying to find out stuff – wait to be shown,' she replied. Was that a look of yearning he could see in her eyes, or was he no longer capable of discerning human emotions?

Later that afternoon Hugo rang Lucy. The line was so clear that her proximity was almost alarming, taking him off his guard as she burst into flurried speech.

'*Time* told me you were alive – but only yesterday. Hugo – I've been frantic. How could you get yourself mixed up in a situation like this again?'

'At the time the bad old days seemed to be the best place to return to.' But he was pleased she sounded so concerned.

'You're blaming me?'

'I didn't say that.'

'Are you hurt?'

'Not significantly. How's Brent?'

'All right.' But there was a change in the tone of her voice – a guardedness that alerted him immediately.

'What's wrong?'

'There's no point in talking about this now.'

'Of course there is.'

'He's – not been too good.'

'What the hell does that mean?' Hugo yelled down the phone.

'He's been absenting himself from St Clouds.'

'Where's he been going?' The fear licked at him.

'The cliffs at Lizard Head. We've all been very concerned.'

'He should be sectioned. Should have been sectioned before. They've got to lock him up.'

'The hospital is very conscious of the problem.' She sounded detached, like a press officer, agitating him even more.

'Is he suicidal?'

'They don't know. I don't know. And there's something else. Someone else.'

'What are you talking about?' The fear swept through him, a wave that kept returning.

'A man came to see him. He convinced the staff that he was a relative and some inexperienced fool allowed him to take Brent out. He was found wandering about on the cliffs – alone.'

'Who *was* this person?'

'I don't know. No one knows. There was a vague description that fitted someone Middle Eastern.'

'An Arab?'

'Perhaps. Why?'

'Has he appeared again?'

'No.'

[91]

'But Brent's been going out on his own since then?'

'Several times.'

'To meet this man?'

'Who knows? He hasn't been seen again.'

'The police were informed?'

'Yes. They have his description – such as it is.'

Eventually Hugo rang off and hurried straight in to Philippa's room.

'Do you think he's suicidal?' she asked bluntly when she had managed to quieten him a little.

'No one seems to know.'

'You have to remember Brent's been in much closer touch with the pyramid than we have. He's been receiving messages for a long time – *and* recording them. Maybe someone's come to listen to him.' She was conscious of her lame conclusion and added, 'God knows who.'

Although they were making no headway, Hugo was delighted that at least they were talking again as they had in the desert, and despite his apprehension he felt a degree of comfort. Was their mental intimacy on its way back? He tried to speak clearly and rationally.

'I know Brent's in danger, Philippa. I have to go back to England – if they'll let us.'

'I think they will,' she replied cautiously, but without a great deal of conviction.

'Will you come with me?'

'Of course.'

'Thank God,' Hugo said with feeling.

'Did you think I wouldn't?' Philippa sounded amazed.

'I don't know. Everything that happened out there in the desert seems so remote now.'

Philippa met his gaze steadily. 'I'm more convinced than ever that what happened out there is of the most vital importance – and is only the beginning. That's why I want to meet Brent.'

'You think he's got the answer?'

'He's closer to it than we are.' She was very certain.

'He *must* be protected. We've *got* to persuade them to let us go.'

'What are we going to tell Ibrahim?' she asked.

'Nothing – until he proves his credentials,' Hugo snapped, conscious that he was no longer in control of anything.

'Maybe he's wondering about ours,' said Philippa.

Tarik Ibrahim arrived the next morning to find Hugo tense and edgy and Philippa calm and reflective. Hugo had phoned Lucy again, only to be told that St Clouds were monitoring Brent carefully and he had not left the building nor had there been any reappearance of his visitor.

He felt torn; on the one hand he longed to be with Brent again, hoping that at last there could be proper communication between them, and on the other he knew instinctively that they would regret leaving the Middle East without returning to the building in the desert, for if he could prove its existence – and its monitors – then he felt he had a grip on something a little more substantial than the spirit world, or whatever it was meant to be.

Their first interview with Ibrahim took place in a small, comfortable lounge. Seated in leather armchairs, they were served with tea and spice cakes whilst Philippa gave an edited account of their escape and subsequent journey from the Iraqi aircraft factory. He listened with studied courtesy, making notes on a pad, rather as if he was a conscientious student at an abstruse lecture.

When she had finished, Hugo asked Ibrahim for news of the Gulf War for they had only been given the vaguest account in the clinic about the allies' advance, but even an event as momentous as this seemed almost irrelevant beside their own experiences.

As he briefed them in more detail on the military develop-ments, Hugo began to detect something of a paradox in Tarik Ibrahim. He had a quiet air of authority that not only gave him considerable stature but also an air of discernment, of perception, but directly he began to ask them questions about the building in the desert Hugo realized there was another aspect to Ibrahim's make-up – the kind of yearning he had associated with Philippa. He could feel its force. Gradually, Hugo understood that he had made a more serious mistake than he had imagined – far bigger

[93]

than he or Philippa had ever realised – in telling Ibrahim the place was a monitoring station; it could delay their repatriation indefinitely. But at least he had already worked out an explanation – one that he hoped would satisfy Ibrahim and blunt his suspicions. He and Philippa had both spent a considerable amount of time trying to produce an authentic alternative to his disastrous comment and were hopeful of being convincing.

Ibrahim was not long in coming to the point. 'You say you went to a monitoring station. Can you explain what you mean?'

'The place was deserted. I assumed it to be doing some kind of surveillance job. There were aerials on the roof and I wondered why it wasn't guarded.'

'Perhaps it was redundant.'

'It didn't look it.'

'Are you sure you're telling me *everything* you know, Mr Fitzroy?' Ibrahim pressed.

'Of course.'

'You didn't, by any chance, go inside?'

'How could we?'

To Hugo's relief Ibrahim tried a new tack. 'You could say your escape – and your journey through the desert – was blessed by Allah.'

'We were lucky.'

'A door blown in, a truck complete with ignition keys, diesel and water? That was lucky indeed. Providential even. Don't you think so, Miss Neville?'

'I guess it can happen.'

'Can it? To me, it's rather as if you had received divine assistance.'

Philippa glanced at him with an assumed ingenuousness. 'We escaped,' she said, deliberately puzzled.

'Rescued?' Ibrahim insisted, still polite, still benign.

'I can assure you that we weren't.' Hugo deliberately sounded as incredulous as possible. Were they coming across, he wondered.

'You do realize that if for any reason you're not telling me the truth my superiors would find it very difficult to allow you to leave.' There was a slight hardening in his voice.

'We *are* telling you the truth. We just got lucky.' Hugo was adamant, but when he looked at Philippa he could feel the tension radiating from her.

'So you stopped at the alleged monitoring station. Why did you do that?'

'We thought there might be some diesel around.' Philippa made an attempt to draw his fire.

'But you were not so lucky *this* time.' He was still watching Hugo.

'No,' she said. 'We couldn't get in.'

'You tried?'

'We rattled the doors.'

We also smashed one in, thought Hugo. Suppose he takes us back there? It would be obvious that the building had been entered – and they would be the first suspects, their fabrications all too clearly exposed.

'No more than that?'

'No more,' said Philippa. 'The place was locked.'

'Suppose we went back there?'

'What on earth for?' Hugo was trying to sound as puzzled and impatient as possible, knowing all the time that he was caught between a need to return and fear of what Ibrahim might find. 'Besides, it's on Iraqi territory,' he added.

'I've already had the area reconnoitred by helicopter,' said Ibrahim firmly. 'We will be perfectly safe. I think you would benefit from retracing your steps. It might work as an *aide-mémoire*.'

Hugo sat on the end of Philippa's bed, the hard sunshine sending a thin beam on to the thick pile carpet. They were both now wondering how much Ibrahim knew – and Hugo had already searched the room, somewhat belatedly, for bugs. There was no immediate evidence of any, but they whispered, just in case.

'We're going to be in trouble when Ibrahim finds evidence of that break-in, there's no doubt about that,' said Philippa.

'We'll deny all knowledge of it.'

'And he'll keep us here until we answer his questions.'

Hugo nodded. Why in God's name had he been so stupid? So careless? 'I don't see what else we can do. He seems determined to take us out there. But there's something about his interest in that building that's – strange. It's as if the place is special to *him* – beyond any military purpose. You can see it in his eyes.'

'Maybe he's like me,' said Philippa.

'What do you mean?'

'I had nothing in my life before all this started. I may be scared shitless of what's going on, but at least – at last – something is.' She looked thrilled and frightened at the same time and Hugo felt shut out. Then Philippa stood up.

'What is it?'

'Look. Can't you see?' She stood sideways against the light and he immediately noticed the change in her – a change that gave him the deep chill of horrified comprehension. Her stomach was slightly distended.

'Listen.'

He knelt down and pressed his ear to her stomach. 'Christ.'

'I'm frightened, Hugo,' she said, 'but I also feel a kind of joy.' She stroked his temple. 'What did you hear.'

Hugo took a while to reply, caught as he was between revulsion and terror. 'It's impossible,' he muttered.

'No. Come on, Hugo, tell me what you heard.'

'The sound of cicadas. As if we were in Provence. But it's – '

'No!' Philippa placed a finger to his lips, and as he looked up he glimpsed the winged serpent in the pupil of her eye.

'You're carrying one of those things – as if it was a baby. As if – '

'It was awakened by our love making.' She was absolutely insistent and, as far as he could tell, totally convinced. Hugo had never been so afraid before – not even when the young boy in the hotel had produced his gun.

'We were talking about reincarnation – not pregnancy,' he whispered. 'Not being host to some mutant.' Hugo's terror was

[96]

blind and childish. Philippa's condition had swept away the last shred of normality and he was once more floundering in a morass of conjecture and uncertainty. 'They should have died out centuries ago,' he added furiously, his mind going off at a tangent, 'not hung on in a form like that. It's vile.'

'Is it? Why should it be?' She was now as angry as he was. 'They don't have any use for human bodies.'

Hugo got to his feet, grabbed Philippa's shoulders and shook her. 'Don't be so stupid.'

'I'm not.' She was more confident now. 'Stop hurting me.'

'We were talking about reincarnation – '

'And we *still* are. Why do you think we've come through the centuries together like this?'

'To understand the change in frequency. To discover when it's going to happen.'

'Is *that* all?' She was still seething but he was not sure that it was just anger.

'What else could there be?'

'We *built* the pyramid. We built the bloody thing! Can't you see? Why are you blinding yourself?'

The sound of the cicadas filled his ears.

'Don't resist the knowledge, Hugo,' she pleaded. 'Don't resist it now – not after all we've been through.'

Hugo struggled to regain logic – if logic was at all possible in this situation. 'There was another reason for the reincarnations? Another reason for us being here?'

'We're powerful, Hugo. Together, we're powerful. In some way I'm going to extend their line. I'm going to strengthen it.'

'This thing will stay on earth when they go?'

'He'll stay.'

'For what purpose?' But he knew. He just wanted to hear her actually say the words.

'He's going to bring about the New Age.' Philippa's voice trembled and Hugo took her in his arms. 'We mustn't fall out now,' she whispered.

'We won't,' he assured her.

*

[97]

Who had taken Brent to the edge of the cliffs, wondered Hugo when he was alone. In addition to the pure spiritual force of the Atlanteans, was there an enemy – a human enemy who was trying to put a halt to their journey to the pyramid? Had what they had seen in the interior of the building in the desert been for their eyes only? Was it merely some kind of orientation point? His head swam with the unanswered questions to such an extent that Hugo developed a blinding migraine in which one single thought began to pound at him incessantly: Brent was in danger; he had to get to him. Yet somewhere behind the pain he knew that first he must return to the desert, at least establish that what they had seen was bricks and mortar. He needed to touch something that was whole, to reassure himself that life hadn't become entirely cerebral. He didn't have Philippa's natural mysticism and still had to claw his way through shards of reality to the light beyond.

Towards evening Ibrahim brought bad news. Once again he had asked Hugo and Philippa to join him in the bland sitting-room with its Western furniture and Islamic aura. 'Your monitoring station in the desert can't be traced,' he told them almost casually.

Hugo was shattered by the statement, not knowing how to respond, and Philippa said nothing. Did she care, he wondered.

'The pilot and his observer are very experienced and they can't find any sign of a building in the area you described.' Ibrahim spoke tolerantly, as if to a recalcitrant child. 'I'm still going to take you out there, though, so that you can see for yourselves.' He spoke with a degree of weary resignation and Hugo thought he might even present them with a bill for the fuel. 'A reconnaissance should satisfy us all, I am sure,' he concluded.

Hugo did not know whether to be relieved or not. Physical evidence of spiritual occurrences might be slipping away from him, but at least the barrier to a return home was down. Protecting Brent was now much more important than searching for evidence.

*

[98]

The sand was bleached out in the night and the moon rode, serene and waxy, over the familiar desolation. Hugo had a feeling of time suspended. Anything was possible out here in this silent wilderness, he thought, as the jeep bucketed its way down the cracked surface of the narrow road.

'It was here,' said Philippa suddenly. 'I'm sure it was.' Ibrahim braked sharply. Hugo stared out indecisively at the darkly rippling sand but she had already clambered down and was running towards some broken masonry. They caught up with her as she was examining a half buried brick. A brick that looked like any other brick. 'I remembered the shape of the sand-hill. It looked like a camel with a couple of humps. I *know* this is the place.'

Ibrahim was impatient for the first time – as if he regretted indulging them. 'How could the Iraqis have demolished a whole base without being seen by our reconnaissance flights?'

'It wouldn't have taken long,' she replied, unaffected by his impatience.

'Any demolition crew would have been seen.' He paused and then came to an abrupt decision. 'You will have to be interrogated in much more detail before I let you both leave our country, Mr Fitzroy.'

'I would like to leave tomorrow – with Miss Neville – as you agreed,' Hugo said quickly. 'I'm sorry about the wasted journey.'

'We are still debriefing,' Ibrahim replied. 'It's all part of the process.' He gave them a polite smile. 'I would like to ask you to take part in an experiment, Mr Fitzroy. Then you will be absolutely free to go.'

'What kind of experiment?' Hugo felt trapped, and his fear about Brent's safety grew until he could hardly bear the pain. His child was in danger. He had to go home.

'You may remember more under hypnosis. Alternatively, you may not. But I'd like you to try. Will you co-operate with me?'

'And if I don't?'

'As you must realize, the last thing I want to do is to delay your return to the UK – '

'In other words, I don't have any choice.'

'Am I expected to undergo this as well?' asked Philippa. She

[99]

put the brick down in the sand, almost burying it, stroking the rough surface lingeringly.

'Just Mr Fitzroy.'

'Why am I singled out?' he asked suspiciously.

'You are a better subject.'

'In what way?'

'You are more open.'

Hugo laughed bitterly. 'You must be the first to say so.'

'You are more open because you are afraid.'

A wave of panic swept him and he stood there in silence, not knowing what to say next, feeling the vast expanse of desert closing in on him, suffocating his mind.

'How on earth do you make that out?'

'I'm experienced at interviewing people, understanding how to put them at their ease.'

Hugo found his quiet authority disconcerting. 'I could still refuse to co-operate.'

'Then you would be our guest for a longer time.'

'My government wouldn't allow that.'

'Perhaps not. But negotiations of this kind do tend to drag on, don't they? Days into months, even into years. If you agree, you can be on a flight to London – '

'How soon?' Hugo cut in sharply.

'The day after tomorrow.'

'And suppose you learn nothing from me?'

'I've always found this process very successful.' He sounded almost complacent.

'Who are you?' Philippa asked abruptly, and both men turned towards her in surprise and consternation. Why is she rocking the boat now, wondered Hugo miserably. Doesn't she care about Brent?

There was a short silence during which Hugo detected a slight and unexpected uneasiness in Ibrahim. Was the desert closing in on him too?

'You know who I am, Miss Neville. I am an intelligence officer.'

'You seem to be on the edge of something else.'

[100]

'Of discovery.' For the first time, there was a degree of menace in his voice.

'Something you might not wish to participate in,' she countered.

'I don't understand.'

She's warning him, thought Hugo. But what was the point? Surely this was the most dangerous move she could possibly make – far worse than his own verbal catastrophe and this abortive trip to a jumble of broken masonry.

'I don't understand,' Ibrahim repeated.

Philippa did not reply.

'We must get back,' he said at last. 'There's nothing to be gained by staying here and talking in riddles, is there?'

As they drove back, Hugo wondered why Philippa had made such a crude accusation. She had obviously detected an uneasiness in Ibrahim, as he had, but surely it would have been better to take a less direct approach. Involuntarily he shivered, a track record of self-deceit passing quickly through his mental landscape. Openness was the only way, he knew that now, but it was hard to break the habit of a lifetime. Ibrahim, though, showed no sign whatever of coming clean. Was he a potential ally or an obstructive enemy?

'Well, Mr Fitzroy. Have you made your decision? Are you going to agree to my process, or not?'

Hugo thought again of Brent and the danger he was in. He had to take the risk.

'I want you to watch this light.'

Ibrahim and Hugo were in a small unfurnished room with two chairs and a light bulb that was large and full of muted colour.

'I want you to try to relax, to look into the light and to listen to my voice. Do you understand?'

'Yes.'

The silence lengthened. Sitting back in his chair, Hugo found some of his tension easing, but he was determined to remain on the defensive and not to allow his mind to drift.

[101]

Ibrahim began to speak in his clear, slightly accented English. 'I want you to take me back over certain aspects of your escape – and subsequent journey through the desert towards Iran. You can visualize the inside of the hangar in the light. Tell me what you see.' He repeated the words again and again, and gradually Hugo lost count of the repetitions, his mind sharpening, becoming clearer, less cloudy. Instead of the hangar, he saw every blade of grass, every detail of the Cornish coast. He was in the bathroom at Lizards, gazing at the objects on the wash stand below the mirror. He was in his study, identifying the books in the library, shelf by shelf. He was in the garden, counting the different kinds of flowers in each bed.

'Focus.'

'What on?'

'You're in the hangar now. Can you see?'

'Yes.' Lizards had vanished.

'How many people are in there?'

'Shall I count?' he asked obediently.

'If you would.'

Hugo saw each of them standing, sitting, talking, even trying to sleep and he counted slowly. 'Fifty-three – including Philippa and me.'

'The officer who met you. Can you see him?'

'Yes.'

'Give me his description.'

Hugo complied.

'Now we move to the building in the desert. Focus. Can you see it?'

'Yes.'

'Did you go inside?'

'No.' He knew he had to fight, but his mind was so clear and he wanted to share the clarity.

'Are you sure?'

'Quite sure.'

'Focus.'

'I am. I can see nothing but colours. Soft colours.'

'Focus.'

'I am.'

'Harder.'

'Nothing.'

But he could see inside the pyramid now. The sunbeam, the winged serpents, the globes, the priests. Everything. So clearly.

'Harder.'

Somehow he resisted, built walls round the images, fought for control. His control. Not Ibrahim's.

'Focus.'

'Nothing.'

'What do you see?'

'I see nothing. I see nothing because I didn't go in. Because *we* didn't go in.'

It would have been so much easier to confide in him, thought Hugo. He'd understand. Ibrahim was trying to help him and he mustn't hold out on him. It wasn't fair. So he'd tell him. The walls of Hugo's fortress were crumbling now and he was reminded of the tide washing over one of the sand castles he had built with Brent in the cove at Tiderace. How they had battled to keep the tide back, father and son working furiously together. But it was no good. Not in the end. Ibrahim was the tide. Ibrahim would win.

'You went *in* there, Hugo.'

That was the first time he had used his first name. Ibrahim was getting closer, lapping at the walls of his fortress.

'You *know* you went in there. What *did* you see?'

Hugo almost capitulated, but Brent ran towards him, yelling excitedly. 'Dad – the tide's on the turn. Keep building. The waves are going back.'

'Am I King Canute?' asked Hugo.

'Are you what?' Ibrahim was completely thrown.

'Am I King Canute?'

'Who?'

'I'm pushing back the waves,' said Hugo.

'No, you're not, Dad,' said Brent. 'The tide's going out. It's going to be OK. The castle walls will stand. They'll stand, Dad. We've beaten the waves.'

'All right,' said Ibrahim wearily. 'We'll stop there, Mr Fitzroy.'

*

[103]

Philippa was waiting for him outside, looking drained and apprehensive, and Hugo's sense of triumph abruptly disappeared.

'There's a call for you – from Lucy. They told me not to
interrupt but I was just about to – '

'What's happened?'

'Speak to her,' she said woodenly.

Hugo broke into a stumbling run, reached his room and
picked up the telephone, already gasping for breath.

'Lucy?'

'I – I had to call.'

'Yes? Yes – what is it?'

'Brent is dead.'

Hugo could not register the words at all. They did not mean
anything.

'I can't hear.'

'I said, Brent is dead. Dead.' Her voice was shrill now. 'Can you
hear me?'

'Yes.' Hugo was shaking so violently that he was barely able to
hold the receiver.

'He killed himself.'

'No.'

'Oh yes, he did.' She was absurdly truculent and self-righteous,
as if he was doubting her word. 'He threw himself over the cliffs
– the one that looks across to the island. To Tiderace.'

'Not there.'

'Yes,' Lucy yelled down the phone. 'There!' She struggled to
control herself. 'I'm sorry to have to tell you this way. He left a
note. He said he couldn't stand the pressure – didn't want to
wake up to another day of it.'

There was a long silence.

'Hugo? Are you there?'

'I'm here.'

'When are you coming home?'

'As soon as I can.' His mind was dull and grey and Hugo felt
that it didn't matter whether he lived or died. Brent. He mouthed
the name. He heard the voice in his mind again. 'The tide's

going out. It's going to be OK. The castle walls will stand, Dad. We've beaten the waves.'

'Brent killed himself – there's not the slightest doubt,' Lucy repeated tonelessly.

'Don't say any more, Lucy, not now.' He didn't want to hear her voice again – didn't want to believe anything she said.

7

EARTH TO EARTH

The graveyard overlooked Tiderace, standing in a bowl-shaped hollow in the cliffs. The church tower was short and stunted but the nave was long and rather grand as befitted the worshipping place of so many wealthy, long-established Cornish families.

The interior of St Lynton's was crowded with members of the hospital staff – nurses, doctors and administrators – as well as a large contingent from the village and friends of the family.

Hugo and Lucy sat in the front pew, facing Brent's coffin just below the altar steps. At the back of the church were a number of reporters and photographers, there to record the headline news of Hugo's release from the Gulf, and the domestic tragedy that had awaited him. He had, however, turned down all requests for television and radio interviews so the rat pack had to content themselves with a sighting only.

Philippa, who had returned from Iran with him, was staying in Bodwell, a small town a few miles up the coast. They had both decided that her presence at the funeral would not be productive, and now, as he stood beside Lucy, he felt grateful that her new partner was also sufficiently tactful to have decided to stay away.

Hugo studied the solid and reassuring face of the Anglican church – so far removed from the Middle Eastern wilderness of uncertainties. The pale stone of the altar, the carvings in the transepts, the stained glass showing Christ and his disciples on a lake, the restrained wall plaques, the muted flowers, the brass engravings on the stone-flagged floor – all gave him a degree of comfort. Here there were no visions of pyramids and winged serpents, no arid desert sand, no beatings and starvation, no ambiguity – nothing but solid sanctuary to the accompaniment of gulls and the pounding of surf on Cornish rock.

His sense of loss for Brent was absolute, and the devastation inside him was increasing – an all-embracing misery that he knew Lucy shared. As the organ began to play Hugo turned his gaze on the natural wood coffin of his only child. A visionary, a dreamer, a guide; his gifts had destroyed him.

After the news of Brent's death there had been no opposition to their return, and he and Philippa had only re-encountered Ibrahim briefly before they left for the airport. He had been conciliatory, seemingly genuinely shocked and concerned at what had happened so far away in England. Hugo was surprised that he had given up and let them go so easily. At the same time, he knew instinctively that the unfinished business between them had to be resumed, although he had no idea how or when.

Once in the air, without any sense of relief at being released, Hugo had wept for Brent and Philippa had made no attempt to comfort him, allowing his grief to spill over in the fortunately near-empty Club Class section of the Boeing.

When he was at last drained of tears, Hugo had said, 'He came to me – during Ibrahim's hypnosis – and told me about our sandcastle and the incoming waves and then the miraculously retreating tide.'

She had been silent for a while. Then Philippa had said, 'If ever I doubted – which I don't think I have – then that's the surest piece of evidence I've heard. You must be so proud of him, Hugo.'

'I let him down badly.'

'Yes – you did. But his love came through – and yours for him. Besides, he's merely discarded one life for another.'

But Hugo had not been able to respond. He felt empty, her words meaningless.

'He'll make contact,' she had persisted. 'I know he will.'

*

As Brent's coffin was lowered into the ground, Hugo and Lucy each dropped a single rose and hurried away, avoiding the vicar, mourners and the press who only managed a few shots whilst they ran towards the car and drove off at high speed. There was to be no wake, no baked meats, nothing – even for those who had travelled long distances and were already looking martyred. Hugo had been adamant and Lucy had readily agreed.

As she drove him through the narrow Cornish lanes, she said, 'I was going to come to Lizards and make you some tea.'

'Not necessary.'

'I don't have to – '

' – get to Tim's house immediately.' Hugo was patient. 'I know – but if you don't mind, I'd rather be alone.'

'That's unlike you,' said Lucy with brutal frankness.

'I've learned to have some inner resources.'

'Out there?' Hugo was silent.

'You don't want to talk about it?'

'I'd rather not,' Hugo replied woodenly.

'I quite understand.' But she sounded as if she did not. 'Can I ask you a question?'

'Of course.'

'Philippa Neville. The woman you shared the experiences with – the one who perhaps helped with the inner resources.' She paused, regretting the cheap remark.

'Yes?' Hugo was too locked up in his own misery to notice.

'Are you friends?'

'Just fellow travellers.'

She changed the subject quickly. 'Did I tell you Brent went back to writing his journal again?'

'No, you didn't tell me. What was he writing about?' Hugo was grateful for her generosity.

'Reincarnation.'

Hugo said nothing, but for a moment a tiny spark of hope sprang up inside him.

As Lucy pulled into the driveway of Lizards, she rummaged on the back seat and produced a crumpled exercise book. 'You'd better take a look.'

'Thank you.'

'I got supplies in, and all the beds have been – ' She broke off, floundering, as Hugo laid a gentle hand on her wrist.

'I'm going to be all right,' he said, as firmly as he could.

Hugo took the exercise book into his study, switched on the electric fire, poured out a large vodka and went to the window, looking out across the cliffs to Tiderace. He would scan the journal and ring Philippa later. It was a gusty evening and the grasses were streaming in the wind; he could almost hear them rustling and rasping above the surging of the sea against the rocks. Rain began to spit over the headland and gradually mist stole across Tiderace, blotting out the foreshore.

After a while he returned to the fire and the chair and the drink. Opening the exercise book with its tightly scribbled pages, he studied it carefully. At first he had some difficulty in understanding the handwriting, but after a while he had the feeling of being drawn into the text.

The Great Pyramid, a survivor of the Flood, was placed at the centre of the earth as a living model of man's destiny to a higher evolution. Once man can centre his solar and magnetic energy and align this energy with the pyramid, he can be synthesized into new forms of light to go beyond our solar system to other star systems in the universe.

The Great Pyramid is part of a universal grid of ancient religious, political and oracular sites. The frequencies of other planets communicate through crystalline sound devices built into the stone passageways between the royal chambers. A calendar is implanted within the steps to the King's Chamber, and the Queen's Chamber has the perfect measurements for deciding the best time to communicate with other worlds.

The Great Pyramid was conceived of by Thoth the Atlantean, and built by Hermes and Isis for the mysteries of space guidance and secrets of impregnable defence. It houses every device needed to calculate the range of stars, the earth's latitude and longitude, the diameter and the thickness of the earth's crust as well as the inner earth.

Atlanteans were sun worshippers and built their temples in the shape of pyramids. Solomon, Moses, Pythagoras and Apollonius were initiated in the Great Pyramid.

The Egyptian Copt historian, Masudi, writing during the Middle Ages, recounted that the Great Pyramid was built during the reign of the sun gods, before the Great Flood, to safeguard ancient knowledge. It was built in limestone to stop erosion before the last geophysical shift. There is evidence that it has experienced one or more floods since fossils and shells from the sea have been found around the base, and indications of salt deposits have been discovered within the Queen's Chamber.

Hermes buried the secrets of Atlantis in the Chamber of Records under the Sphinx and the pyramid to be found before the next shift in the earth's axis. The passageways between the two chambers record the ages of man upon the earth and predict the total numbers of years yet remaining before the new millennium.

The earth is a gigantic magnet charged with electromagnetic force. Many prehistoric remains of buildings, walls and roads were once part of a planned instrument extending over parts of Great Britain and the rest of the world, as a means of marking and channelling lines of electromagnetic force.

There is a startling resemblance between the ruins of the Inca and the Cyclopean ruins in Italy, Greece and different parts of the world. They may have belonged to the same world culture to not only mark but to control the magnetic field of the earth.

Legends of space and cosmic exploration appear to have been current in the most remote periods of recorded civilization. According to the Secret Doctrine, based on the Stanzas of Dyzan, science does not deny the presence of man on earth from great antiquity, though that antiquity cannot be determined since that presence is conditioned on the unascertained age of geological periods. But mankind came

[110]

from the stars, not from the primeval slime of earth, and has developed into the form now familiar to us. Men and women were not always of that shape. They were Atlanteans – wholly different from their human progeny.

Zecharia Sitchin unearthed evidence in the Earth Chronicles of a superior race of beings who once inhabited our world; travellers from the stars who arrived aeons ago and planted the genetic seed that would ultimately blossom into mankind.

There are references to space flights, space vehicles, and fairly accurate descriptions of how earth would look from space, again connected with gods and supernatural heroes. Descriptions in Indian writings of powered aircraft, air attacks on cities, radiation and radar, would be unbelievable had they not been written before their modern counterparts came into existence.

According to Barbara Marciniak and the Pleiadians, earth is a cosmic library – a free-will zone, designed to be an intergalactic exchange centre of information shared through frequencies of the genetic process. The earth is a highway for energies to travel to our space zone – easy to reach from one galaxy to another.

Hugo paused to switch on the light, his head reeling with Brent's prose, but aware there was something very authoritative about the Journal.

Thoth-Hermes came from Orion and materialized on earth approximately one and a half million years ago. He was able to communicate by thought and disassembled and reassembled the atoms and molecules of objects, lifting them from one place to another. Through this once simple method we have giant heads on Easter Island, the Great Pyramid of Egypt and other remnants of far greater civilizations than we know today.

Thoth conquered the knowledge of the laws of time and space and his wisdom made him ruler over various Atlantean colonies, including the Mayans.

[111]

Thoth took the Lemurians who wanted scientific power to an island continent named Atlantis. There they began to build a great technical civilization, linking their minds together and projecting holographic images which gradually solidified, took form and became real. It was not long before they started to export their civilization and wanted to rule not only the Lemurians, but the spirits of nature, the devas and the elementals. Under Thoth's rule the consciousness of his scientists grew darker, and their abuse of nature eventually changed the earth's balance and was to destroy this advanced civilization.

It was inevitable that war developed between the Atlanteans and the Lemurians, but also between the Atlanteans and nature. Thoth and his scientists created a crystal so finely chiselled as to absorb the sun's rays for a new form of energy. There was an ample supply of quartz and for many years they experimented with various sizes until they captured nature's secret of collective energy and smaller crystals began to propel small objects.

In the centre of the capital of Atlantis, Poseidonis, a great event took place between the seven leaders in the Great Pyramid.

Thoth visualized a form, a structure, and commanded his scientists to create the present form of man. They had seven models to work from which would represent the seven races. There is still in existence a crystal skeleton buried in South America which was the original blueprint for the human race as we know it today.

Thoth said to his creations, 'Go to new lands and I will give you great power.'

Thus the struggle that began on Orion continued on earth, matching the narrative of good and evil recounted in the Bible. The story of Cain and Abel is the story of Sananda and Thoth, each competing for their version of the truth – the truth of love and light, or the truth of reason and technology. This was not a physical struggle, it was a struggle of thoughts and ideas.

[112]

Mentally exhausted, Hugo rested again, walking to the window, looking out on to the misty headland. Brent. Which dark stranger had been commissioned to execute his son?

Eventually Hugo returned to the journal and was riveted by the next few sentences.

In the 1980s, through the agency of the Brotherhood of the Winged Disc, the Atlanteans contacted the Arab Federation, anxious to discover the identity of the reincarnation of Thoth. But they had no knowledge.

The presence of the Atlanteans on earth has always been protected by the Brotherhood of the Winged Disc, based in the Middle East. Some members, however, in this generation have become self-interested and wish to harness the Atlanteans' power for the military purposes of the Arab Federation.

Now the Atlanteans are to leave earth at last, knowing their influence is needed elsewhere. They await the date of the change in the earth's frequency that according to tradition can only be found in the Chamber of Records underneath the pyramid by Thoth or his designates, for only they can penetrate the chamber. Saddam Hussein, however, has pressurized members of the Disc to tell the Atlanteans that the discovery of the date is not just the prerogative of the delegates of Thoth. He has already searched the pyramid in great detail to no effect, but is still claiming that he can release the Atlanteans. In their desperation, and with the lack of any other obvious alternative, they are inclined to believe the Iraqi leader. In exchange for their escape they have promised to provide the Arab Federation with a formula for a particularly toxic nerve gas that could decimate thousands – a formula that could be made in laboratories in the Middle East and was originally developed for the protection of Atlantis.

Hugo put the exercise book down. The significance of what they had to do overwhelmed him completely. Their journey, hardly begun, had to be completed.

Resolutely, Hugo returned to the last paragraph in the journal.

In the event of my premature death I designate my father, Hugo Fitzroy, and his companion, Philippa Neville, as the representatives of Thoth. They share the vision and its responsibilities.

There was no more. Just a neat line under the word 'responsibilities'. Hugo sat staring at the text. Then he went back to the window and gazed out yet again at the darkness. The mist had lifted and he could just see the rocks at the lowest point of Tiderace. Was that a boy waving to him? Was that his son?

Philippa answered the phone immediately and he guessed straight away that she felt shut out. Feeling guilty for not having phoned her earlier, Hugo hurriedly explained the significance of what he had read the previous night. She heard him out without comment.

'I'd like you to come here and read this for yourself.'

'Now the Gulf War's over,' she said, 'maybe Saddam will be executed – or assassinated.'

'There'll be someone to take over if he is,' Hugo responded with bleak certainty. 'His death won't make the slightest difference to any bargains struck in the pyramid.'

'I can hardly believe any of this,' she muttered, and he wondered if she was experiencing what he had felt: belief was more difficult here, in the mundanity of the UK, than it had been in the emptiness of the desert. 'It's hard to accept the vastness of it all – the responsibilities we've got,' she said slowly. 'Winged serpents with nerve gas? It's so bizarre, completely absurd. Yet I know it's for real, as sure as I know what a Safeways supermarket trolley looks like. What's more – it's moving inside me, Hugo. All the time. And I heard its voice reaching me in the night.'

'For God's sake – '

'It's true, Hugo. When are you going to accept it's all true? How much more evidence do you need? You can't go on doubting

– not any more.' She was shouting down the phone now, and he wondered if she was trying to drown her own lack of faith.

'I'm sorry.' He had to reach her. 'I find it very hard to swim with this tide. But I'm trying. What did the voice say?'

'I woke up round about dawn and I felt it move inside me. Then I heard something saying "I must grow inside you, enter your mind, lead you to the final destination. But only you can find the chamber."' Philippa began to cry. 'Every damned word keeps repeating in my head – all the time. What am I going to do? It's as if I've taken over from Brent. Did he have one of these creatures inside him? Dictating what the hell he had to do?'

Hugo tried to speak calmly, acutely aware of her pain and corroding sense of isolation. 'Do you want me to collect you from the hotel?'

'Come quickly.'

'I'll start out now. I'm not trying to hide from any of this. You do realize that, don't you?'

'How can either of us hide? With this thing inside me?'

'It began on Tiderace. We have to get there. Then we'll know where we have to go.'

As Hugo drove down the coast road he tried to cling to the banal normality of the shops and filling stations, cafés and pubs as he sped past them. They were the familiar world that was to give way to the unfamiliar – the parallel life that he had begun to inhabit with Brent and then with Philippa and now with them both. It was becoming increasingly impossible to avoid the knowledge that the Atlanteans had always lived alongside the material world and that he himself had already inhabited many other lives. The thought of his present responsibilities deeply depressed him; evasion was still second nature. Could he change, be different, as Brent had said? And then there was Philippa. If one of the creatures was really growing inside her it could have the most sinister implications. What would it become? What would it make her become? Could she be hosting a monster?

The Happy Eater, Shell Select, the Fortune of War, Little Chef, Toyota, the Spread Eagle, Esso, Brabazon Motors, Oak Rooms

Tea House, the Singing Kettle, Busy Lizzie Garden Centre, West Cliff Farm Shop, Honeypot B & B – the safety of the familiar names was precious, their speeding litany a sanctuary of the material world. The sun was shining brightly after yesterday's mist and the sea was a brilliant blue, but the unknown was waiting for him. He saw something move on the surface of the water which reminded Hugo of a long tentacle. They were drawing him in and he was leaving the rational behind. From Tiger Tokens to infinity, he thought involuntarily.

8

SPIRIT GUIDE

The September sea was gentle, small waves slapping the sides of the boat as Hugo ferried Philippa towards the island, the outboard chugging noisily, seemingly the only sound in a blanket of silence.

When he had brought her back to Lizards the previous day they had made love, and despite the thing inside her the result was even better than their previous experience in the desert. Hugo was amazed to feel complete unification, and with a surge of unfamiliar joy knew that he could rely on the fact that the eternity of their relationship had been reaffirmed once again – and those doubts at least could finally be dismissed.

Slowly, throughout the long day and night, Hugo and Philippa had accepted that in Brent's absence they were destined for a mission. They also knew that their reincarnation was at the core of it all and that they had been developing over the centuries, heading towards the pyramid. The age of miracles was not dead, Hugo had told himself, and a few lines of Schopenhauer returned to him: 'Every parting gives a foretaste of death; every coming together again a foretaste of the resurrection.' He had held Philippa tightly in his arms and at last they had both slept.

Now as the old chine-built boat ploughed towards the rocky outcrop of Tiderace, Hugo felt a sense of finality – that by taking Philippa here they would draw closer to the spirit of Brent and see the way ahead at last. Briefly Lucy's face swam into his consciousness and he felt a stab of pain. They had not spoken for over a week. And how well did he know Philippa? How well did she know him? They still seemed to be holding back personally, not examining sufficiently the experiences they had shared.

'Sometimes I feel we've been travelling through all those centuries as strangers,' said Hugo suddenly. 'We're like the pyramid – full of hidden chambers.'

She agreed, and there was an uneasy silence while each waited for the other to begin.

With considerable pain, Hugo began to tell Philippa about his parents, their self-destruction and how he had never been able to face up to those childhood horrors. 'I reinvented myself – and made a total balls-up of everything in the process. All self-invention does is ring-fence a void. It means you can't relate to people – unless they've seen the abyss, too.'

Philippa did not respond quickly. She seemed, like him, to be wondering whether she could really expose her innermost being. Then she began in a rush, her words frantic, tumbling over each other in a determined attempt at final exorcism. 'I can under-stand that, Hugo. My parents may have been stable but they occupied an island – and all I had was a tiny atoll. I yearned to be loved, but at first I could only relate to other women – lack of mother-love, my analyst told me – so my first sexual relationship was with a woman. We lived together and were in love – were physical lovers. Does that repel you?'

'Why should it?' The island was in sight now, beguilingly gentle in the gathering sunshine. 'Don't be afraid, Philippa. You know how much I love you.' He watched a cormorant diving low into the water, searching for fish. 'Did you break up?' he said softly.

'Mary died. We thought it was migraine, but the doctor insisted she went for a scan.'

'Cancer?'

'A brain tumour. She left me a couple of weeks later.' Philippa swept on quickly but her agony reached him. 'After Mary I began to have rather halting relationships with men.'

'How long did your time with Mary last?' he asked gently.

'Five years. A long time.' The painful, staccato statements seemed almost forced out of her now. 'I was writing and she was

[118]

a painter. We lived in a valley in Vermont which was very remote. We became recluses. We were self-sufficient. Didn't need anyone else. But all the time I was waiting.'

'Waiting for what?'

'For it to end.' She sounded slightly impatient, as if he ought to know. 'I knew it was going to end – that it was only an interval.'

'Did you see the pyramid?'

'No.' There was a long pause as Tiderace towered above them. 'When it's over, if we survive – survive as we are now – could we find a valley or a desert or some place where we can be together just for a while without moving on?'

Hugo nodded. 'I would hope it won't be an interval, though. That we could be permanent.' Permanency – it was something he'd always shied away from, subconsciously avoiding a prolonged intimacy that could be revealing. It was different now; he'd come such a long way in a very short time. But even as he acknowledged it, he felt an onrush of panic. Who knew what could possibly happen with the thing inside her and their mutually impossible goal.

'What will happen when – when this is born, Hugo? Will I be released?' She sounded dependent on his reply.

'You'll be protected,' he said, as comfortingly as he could.

'Who by?'

'By me.'

'And if you aren't enough?' she asked baldly.

'The Atlanteans.'

'They are a little ambiguous, aren't they? They only want to leave and they don't care how they do it; they don't care what harm comes to anyone, whether it's the enemies of the Arab Federation – or us. How can they care, Hugo? They're neither good nor evil. They're completely amoral.'

'We'll see this through together,' he said doggedly.

'If we *do* die – we'll be sharing another life.'

'Will we? That sounds just a little too cosy, don't you think? We've been preparing for this for a long time. Isn't this meant to be the end?'

*

The boat gently grounded on the sloping shelf that led to the cove. The sunshine seemed old and mellow and warm as they stepped ashore, wading through shallow water and then on to firm sand and rock.

'We'll climb to the top of the cliff,' said Hugo.

'Do you hope to see the pyramid?' She sounded more cheerful, as if his fatalism had in some way comforted her.

'I don't know. Everything began here. That's why we've come.'

The bullet whistled over their heads and embedded itself in the rock.

'Get down.'

Philippa dragged Hugo behind an outcrop of rock. There was another whine and this time the water rippled behind them.

'Get back in the boat,' he whispered.

Another shot cracked out, followed by a spreading silence.

'Don't move yet.'

'I wasn't going to.'

Suddenly there were more shots – three this time and then a fourth. Gulls rose screaming and flew high over their heads. The terrible silence spread again.

'I'm going to check this out.'

'No – '

'I'll stay flat against the rock,' Hugo muttered, inching himself forward.

'Dad.'

He froze.

'Dad.'

The voice *must* be inside his head.

'Who's that?'

'No one.' Hugo felt the chill spreading.

'I heard a child's voice.'

'Keep quiet.'

'Dad.'

Hugo moved cautiously around the rock. Now he could see the beach again, his heart racing so fast that the pounding was unbearable.

Brent was there, wearing khaki shorts and a sun hat, younger than he had seen him before. His chest was bare and brown, he wore unmistakable Clarks sandals and clutched a bucket and spade.

'Dad.'

'What is it?'

'You're to go.'

'Where?'

'You'll come back this time, won't you?'

'Of course,' Hugo stuttered.

'I've made a castle.'

But he hadn't – he'd made a pyramid.

Brent's body was translucent now, and through his hazy outline Hugo could see a man lying, half in and half out of the sea. Most of his head had been shot away and a cloud of blood moved with the waves.

'I've made a castle.' The voice was becoming fainter.

'It's a pyramid.'

Brent turned to look wonderingly at the pile of sand which glowed when struck by a shaft of sunlight. Then his body shimmered and grew even more insubstantial until what appeared to be a burnt-out negative hovered briefly and then disappeared.

The body lay in the lapping breakers. It wore jeans and a white shirt and the features were those of an Arab.

Hugo was flattened against the rock, rooted, unable to move. Then he heard steps on the shingle.

'Hugo Fitzroy.'

The voice was vaguely familiar, but in his sweating bewilderment Hugo had no sense of recognition, only a paralysing terror.

'Hugo Fitzroy.'

Nausea swept over him and he swayed on his feet, praying that he wasn't going to pass out, hanging on to the rock grimly until his fingers stung. He mustn't fall. He mustn't go under. Not now. Not with both their lives at stake.

[121]

'Philippa Neville.'

The voice was slightly accented, authoritative, expectant.

Hugo stepped out of his inadequate hiding-place to see Tarik Ibrahim, perfectly groomed, his dark beard lustrous and his grey suit uncrumpled. Only his light-brown shoes were slightly scuffed. In his hand he still held a small automatic weapon.

'You were walking into an ambush.'

'What ambush?' He felt light-headed and slightly dizzy. The waves made little lapping noises as they nuzzled the corpse.

'Iraqi Intelligence.'

'What the hell are they doing here?' asked Philippa.

'Trying to kill you.'

'Then who *are* you?' Hugo asked. 'You don't represent a government, do you?'

'No – I belong to the Brotherhood of the Winged Disc. I hope you'll forgive my charade. I was not sure of you; there were things I needed to know – still need to know, particularly as I'm sure you managed to resist my powers of hypnotism. I was a little mortified by that. I didn't realize how many inner resources you had to fall back on.'

I didn't know then, thought Hugo. But I do now. He looked down at the corpse, watching the cloud of blood disperse as the tide advanced. Ibrahim here? His presence seemed to be impossible. All the worlds were crumbling now – Tiderace, the Pyramid, the desert – and now the Brotherhood.

'He'd been sent to kill you,' said Ibrahim. He was very calm, as courteous as before but somehow rather fatherly and protective. How many more parts can he play, wondered Hugo.

'How did he know where we were?'

'He only had to read the papers. You rather caught the headlines. He'd had you under surveillance for a couple of days. When you set out for the island he chartered a boat and came in from the eastern side.'

'And you?'

'I saw him go.'

'So you'd been watching him watching us.'

'I'm here to protect you both. To tell you we are ready.'

'Ready for what?' Hugo felt a stab of fear. He tried to take a grip on himself; at least Ibrahim was an earthly representative.

'To guide you to the pyramid,' Ibrahim was saying. 'I'm satisfied about your identity now – and there's really no point in delaying any further.'

'Why didn't you tell us before?' Philippa demanded.

'Because I wasn't sure what you knew – and what you'd seen. None of us were. We couldn't be absolutely certain you were the two people we'd been waiting for.'

'How many of you are there?' asked Hugo.

'A few. As you must appreciate, the Atlanteans are regarded by us as a sacred trust. They are part of Islam. They have wanted to leave for a long time now – and we are anxious to help them.' He paused. 'But we can do nothing without you.'

Hugo was not prepared to admit anything. Not yet. 'I don't know what you're talking about. It's absolute madness – '

'No, Mr Fitzroy. It is not madness. We are sure now that you are both reincarnates – light walkers. You would not have come here if you weren't. This was the source, wasn't it? The island was the beginning of recognition. But let me prove it to you. Your son did *not* take his own life – he was assassinated by Iraqi Intelligence, just as you would have been had I not protected you.' Hugo tried to speak but Ibrahim had already turned away.

They followed him to the top of the cliffs, Ibrahim walking a few yards ahead. No one spoke as the seabirds wheeled around them and Hugo felt a gathering sense of completeness. The turf was short and springy beneath his feet and he kept recognizing little memories of Brent when he was a child – memories which so far had eluded him. Then, as they emerged from the rock shadow, the image of the pyramid glowed in hard sunlight, etched into a background of brilliant blue sky. There were no clouds, not the breath of a breeze; the perfect geometric image.

*

As they stood there, Philippa began to shake and Hugo tried to take her in his arms, but she gently pushed him away.

'It's so beautiful,' she said. 'So utterly benign.'

'Yes,' Ibrahim agreed. 'It is. But you have to remember the Atlanteans are desperate. They believe in no one – neither you nor the Iraqis.' He turned to Hugo. 'You don't doubt me now, do you?'

Hugo didn't know what to reply. Should he still have doubts? The immensity of it all almost overwhelmed him.

'Yes,' he said at last. 'We are who you hope we are. And we *were* shown the pyramid.'

'How did the Iraqis find out about the Atlanteans?' Hugo asked, relieved to have another confidant at last.

'As you can understand, the secret of their existence was very closely guarded, but regrettably the Brotherhood was infiltrated by the Iraqis.'

'For how long?'

'A year. Perhaps longer.'

'Will the Atlanteans give Iraq this nerve gas formula?'

'They will agree to do so if you don't arrive soon – and obviously if you are not successful. Then only Allah can help the Kurds, the Marsh Arabs, the Israelis.'

'Can't the Brotherhood intervene?'

'What could they do? I am sure you understand you must travel to the pyramid at once.'

'Where is it?' asked Philippa.

'Egypt.'

'And how can we possibly trust you?' Hugo was shaken by another wave of doubt.

Ibrahim gazed up at the image of the pyramid. 'Would *that* appear if I was your enemy?'

But neither Hugo nor Philippa could be sure.

'I can guarantee you'll be given protection.'

'I don't see we have any choice,' said Philippa.

'You must come with me now.'

'We need some time here together first. We must talk this over alone.'

'I can give you half an hour.' Ibrahim was brusque. 'I'll respect your privacy, but I shan't be far away. You must learn to trust me, both of you.'

'That'll take some time.'

'Don't let it take too long.' Tarik Ibrahim walked slowly away until he was lost to sight on the steep path. The edges of the pyramid became blurred and gradually began to fade.

'Hold me.' Hugo took Philippa's hand. 'Hold me tightly. I want to feel our strength. We're going to need so much of it.'

But all he could actually feel was her swollen stomach.

They lay on the hard, flinty ground, wrapped in each other's arms, while the sun seemed to become as searingly hot as it had been in the desert.

'Look.' Philippa stared up into the intensity of heat. The beam sprang out, gilding their bodies, filling them with desire. She placed her lips on his and, almost instantly, Hugo saw their lives come hurtling at him, diffused images that terrified him in their enormity. A crystal pyramid shattered by a tidal wave, a huge serpent twisting in its death throes, dog-headed men, a black dragon, the tree of knowledge, a winged disc, a bronze Zeus, warrior gods descending bloodied from a fiery heaven, the Grail shimmering in an unearthly light, the pyramid of Giza dominating everything. Then through its portal he caught glimpses of war – was shivering in a trench that stank of human defecation and corruption. Rats ran through the soiled water under his feet and the guns blazed on the near horizon, the shells bursting over his head, lighting up the charnel house of a no man's land that lay behind the wire. A dead man nestled against him, his skull split from ear to ear, his mouth open in a grinning rictus. Merciful darkness came and then he was conscious of Philippa somewhere near at hand.

[125]

'What are you doing here?'

'Nursing.'

'What's happening?'

'You're dying, Hugo. But there'll be rebirth. As always – until we've finished the journey.'

'Where?'

'At the pyramid.'

'Is that death final?'

'Who knows?'

The scene vanished, but he felt he was being suffocated. Then he knew that she was beside him, her lips sealing his, the thing inside her thrusting at him.

This time it was Hugo's turn to push her gently away, and they lay side by side, sweating in the beam.

'It's so powerful.'

'The beam?' she asked.

'Your child,' he replied.

Philippa shuddered. 'It's not my child,' she protested. 'It can't be.'

But they both knew that it was.

9

EGYPT

The privately chartered Egyptian jet left from Stansted the next day. Hugo, Philippa and Ibrahim shared luxurious cabin space while in less distinguished accommodation half a dozen young men sat around smoking and playing cards. They all had an air of quiet professionalism. Hugo had seen the breed before in the service of celebrities and politicians. Minders. Bodyguards. They made him feel both safe and exposed at the same time. God knows, he thought, I should have got used to all this, but the other lives – if they *were* other lives – still only had the substance of a half-remembered dream. And this life was too precious now, with Philippa, to even contemplate death.

Hugo leant back in his seat, closing his eyes, considering recent events. There was no doubt in his mind that he and Philippa had an overwhelming responsibility and that it could only be fulfilled if they reached the pyramid. Ibrahim was an ambivalent figure but they needed him. At the very least he must be a member of the Winged Disc; the pyramid was proof of that. They had returned from Tiderace together, throwing the corpse of their potential assassin overboard when they were certain that they could not be seen by any other craft. It had been an incredible moment – the disposing of an anonymous human being as a piece of detritus.

Once ashore, Ibrahim had explained to the bewildered boat-yard staff that they would have to go out to the island to reclaim their boats as 'our small party had to be cancelled because of a lady's illness.' The enigmatic announcement was accompanied by the passing over of a large amount of 'recovery fees', all of which were accepted without question. The situation had been farcical but no one had seen the funny side. All three of them had then returned to Lizards and they had told Ibrahim everything they could remember about the interior of the building in the desert. In return, he had explained that the highly sophisticated monitoring system belonged to the Iraqis and he suspected there might be others in other remote regions. Their presence must have been detected by a hidden camera, he had continued, and so the building had been quickly dismantled at night.

Ibrahim kept an armed watch through the sleepless night, and Hugo and Philippa had lain together in the large double bed in the guest-room, for neither wanted to encroach on Lucy's territory.

'Should we really have confided in Ibrahim – just like that?' Philippa had asked, 'And why didn't the Iraqis come for us?' She was clearly unconvinced. 'We were easy targets in the desert.'

'Too easy,' Hugo had surmised. 'I guess they wanted to know what we were going to do next. After all, they had nothing to do with our easy escape.'

Philippa had agreed. 'I don't think the Iraqis got wise to us until we were amongst the computers. Maybe they're using us.'

'So you *do* suspect Ibrahim?'

'We shouldn't trust anyone,' she had replied uncertainly. 'Don't forget what he said – the Disc was penetrated by the Iraqis. We've no idea where he stands in all this.'

But Hugo had been adamant. 'He could summon up the pyramid, couldn't he? He must know that Tiderace is a receiver. Brent was the original recipient, of course. We can see, too, but not as clearly. The same applies to Ibrahim.'

'That's not a guarantee of his loyalty to the Atlanteans, is it?'

'Surely they wouldn't give him this – this second sight if he was working against them?'

Philippa had shrugged. 'Why should we assume the Atlanteans have any moral concepts? They want to go – and they don't care who releases them. Hence the gas for the lucky winner. Oh yes, Hugo, you really can't be an idealist over this. If we wanted

[128]

something like that – and they had the power to give it to us – I'm sure we could name our price. They're trapped, and unless we can discover that frequency they'll remain so.'

'Don't they realize the Iraqis have *no* way of finding it? That only *we* can help them?'

'Clearly that's not a concept they can grasp.'

'If they can communicate telepathically, doesn't that give them a reasonable chance of understanding what's in other people's minds?'

'I don't know. Why should it?'

'This is incredible,' he had complained. 'I feel driven, but where?'

'They're a higher intelligence,' she had replied. 'But a higher intelligence with limitations. After all, they can't engineer their own escape like they engineered ours. We're their guides, aren't we – just as much as they've been ours?'

'And the Iraqis?'

'They haven't succeeded so far. We're the unknown quantities. That's why the Atlanteans want to give us a chance. Ibrahim may be their loyal servant, accepting them as gods; he may, on the other hand, only see them as providers.'

'They won't pass on the nerve-gas formula if the Iraqis can't get them airborne.' But Hugo had known he was clinging to a straw.

'There's very little time left. We have all the right qualifications for the job – the most distinguished lineage of time travel – but if we don't show up, then there are only the Iraqis left.'

'They're hardly likely to accept that,' Hugo had persisted.

'I think you'll find they'll accept anything. Maybe even give them an inducement payment. I can sense urgency and desperation. I can sense that in myself, Hugo.'

'We're part of them,' he had replied, and had immediately felt appalled at the idea. 'Are we leaving with them?'

'The Iraqis won't find the frequency, I'm sure of that.' Philippa was following her own line of thought.

'No. But they'll claim they will. And if we're dead –' Hugo had paused – 'I should think the Iraqis might well convince the Atlanteans to pass across the formula to their scientists – without delivering the goods.'

[129]

'Could they be *that* trusting?'

'They're that desperate.'

'So are we going with Ibrahim? With all these reservations?'

'We have to.'

'He could kill us himself.'

'He could, but why then did he go through that elaborate charade today?'

Philippa had stared at him without replying and Hugo had added grimly, 'Put it like this, if he's with us, then he killed our assassin. If he's not, the assassin was out to kill him and almost succeeded. It just isn't possible to resolve Ibrahim's ambiguities. Not yet. But there can be no freedom for us if we try to escape our responsibilities. And like it or not the Atlanteans *are* our responsibilities.'

'Suppose we die?'

'Then we'll be free in another life.'

'Isn't that too glib?' Philippa had asked angrily. 'What about the Atlanteans? They're ageless, timeless. They can wait.'

'For another change in frequency?' Hugo had been dismissive. 'They won't see that.'

'But why?' she had asked anxiously, defensively.

'If they don't get freedom, they'll wither away. Just as we were about to do. They need renewal – like we did. We got it through each other.'

She had nodded, knowing he was right, and Hugo became even more convinced through her acceptance. Whatever side Tarik Ibrahim was on, they had to move ahead.

Later on, they had made love and when the love-making was finished, Philippa and Hugo had slept; in their dreams they had risen with the Atlanteans towards the opening portal of the pyramid and up into the dawn. Half waking, Hugo had the curious sensation that they and the Atlanteans were indivisible, and just on the point of oblivion he remembered the Latin saying *'Flectere si nequeo superos Acheronta movebo.'* 'If I cannot move the gods, I will stir up hell.' Who was going to do that, he wondered. The Iraqis? The Federation? The Brotherhood?

'Or us?' asked a voice in his mind.

*

Hugo had only slept for an hour or so, and when he had awoken again he had been filled with mocking logic, his conversation with Philippa dissolving into ludicrous fantasy. How had he ever managed to convince himself that those winged serpents were gods, and past reincarnations had put him on their level? Self-renewal was fair enough, abandonment of alcohol a necessity, but did he have to believe in fairies? He had lain there, letting the grey English morning attack him, but when he had remembered in detail all that had happened, Hugo had soon been enmeshed in the spiritual world again, leaving reason behind, knowing it to be the bar to freedom.

Now, in the jet, Hugo gave up his halting attempts to sleep and turned to Ibrahim.

'Do you have an itinerary?' he asked drily. 'Or is it all still a mystery tour?'

'A magical mystery tour,' corrected Ibrahim with a slightly ponderous attempt at humour. 'I shall take you to the Brother-hood's headquarters in Cairo – and then we shall go to the pyramid of Giza. There will be maximum security.'

'What happens when we get to the pyramid?'

'We shall take you both to the Chamber of Records. The rest is hopefully up to you.'

'Of course – you do realize we have no idea what to do,' Philippa interposed.

'I'm sure you will be guided into doing what is best. Naturally you will meet my companions first.'

'How long will that take?' asked Philippa.

'An hour. No longer.'

'And how far is the pyramid?'

'A considerable distance into the desert. We shall arrive there late tonight.'

During the remainder of the flight, Hugo and Philippa both tried, in their separate ways, to get to know Ibrahim better, and to understand his involvement with the pyramid and the Brotherhood. As a result of their determined but slightly over-casual questioning, he told them his life story, but Hugo was not entirely convinced.

'My parents were wealthy Iranian lawyers,' Ibrahim began, 'both with an Oxford education but still committed Muslims. They had a foot in both worlds: the veneer of Western sophistication and the devout heart. Soon after I came home from Oxford the Shah was deposed, the Ayatollah came to power and Islamic law was dramatically enforced. I wasn't sure if I could embrace it as willingly as my parents had, and it didn't take me long to realize I couldn't – so I became a closet liberal, assumed to be as strictly religious as my parents. I thought I'd bide my time, wait for the regime to change, to become less fundamentalist. Then I realized that this wasn't going to happen, and while I was still wavering, trying to decide what to do, my father became terminally ill. He summoned me to his bedside in the traditional manner, but I was alarmed to find that he was desperate to tell me something. At first I put his bizarre, wholly unbelievable story down to the ramblings of a dying man – just as you, Mr Fitzroy, put your son's journal down to madness. Anyway, he took my hands in his and said he was going to tell me the greatest secret in the world. I waited, horrified by what I thought was his mental deterioration.' Ibrahim paused, looking at a small stain on the carpet. He examined the mark for a long time before resuming, and Hugo tried to work out whether this was a calculated act or he was genuinely gathering his thoughts. Then, more hesitantly, he continued.

'He told me that in the pyramid of Giza there lived gods who were also called Atlanteans. They had great powers and had arrived centuries before by the grace of Allah. They were committed to spiritually empower Islam, to underpin the most glorious revolution of all, to create unity of heart and profound spirituality throughout the Arab world. They would not always be present, however; they had intimated that they had work to do elsewhere and that their time on earth was limited. In due course, strangers would come from outside the faith, time travellers, light walkers, who were destined to enter the Chamber of Records and to discover the time when the earth would change its frequency and the space portal would open. Only then would the Atlanteans be free to leave.'

Was he to be believed or was he putting up a smoke-screen? Hugo didn't have the slightest idea, and he could see that Philippa was just as perplexed.

Ibrahim resumed. 'Although I'm deeply concerned about the fanaticism of my people, I know the faith is strong enough to allow the departure of the Atlanteans. Besides, their existence was for many centuries kept secret by the Brotherhood. My father told me that I would be permitted one sighting only in my lifetime.'

'And have you had that sighting?' asked Philippa, suddenly showing real interest.

'Yes. I was taken to the pyramid by Jamal – one of the elders of the Brotherhood. He and his forebears have taken the role of Magi – revealers and communicators. It is Jamal's responsibility to call the Atlanteans from the casket.'

'The casket?'

'The place where they meditate and pray. I waited outside until Jamal called me. When I entered he was standing there with one of them hovering above him in a globe.'

'This Atlantean – ' said Hugo, 'did he look more like a winged serpent than a god?'

'How can we say what a god should look like?' said Ibrahim pompously.

'Did you communicate?'

'It was the most glorious moment of my life. I felt a sense of power and commitment, and sure and certain knowledge that Islam would be protected, whether the Atlanteans were present in the pyramid or not.' He spoke so passionately that Hugo was deeply moved. If this was a fabrication then Ibrahim was a brilliant actor.

'Is that all?'

'Isn't that enough?'

'If they are so powerful,' said Hugo, 'why do they have to bargain for their release?' He was determined to play the devil's advocate and test out Ibrahim's belief.

'Because they are afraid.'

'When they are so strong?'

'If they can't be released I suspect they may lose power and wither away.'

'Have you evidence of that?'

'Yes. My father showed me a photograph of a dead Atlantean. One who had dried out. It looked like a fallen angel.' Ibrahim's eyes filled with tears and once again Hugo felt genuinely moved.

'How did an Iraqi get into the pyramid?' asked Philippa, assuming a more aggressive role.

'There are representatives of each Arab country in the Brotherhood. It was his right.'

'And he corrupted the Atlanteans?' she asked.

'He offered them a chance – although it was, of course, quite false.'

'And the Atlanteans weakened,' muttered Hugo. 'So despite their power, they have human feelings – these gods of yours. They know fear – and death.'

'They were once human.'

Does he guess, as we do, that they were once like us, wondered Hugo, and yet despite their powers they lacked our gift of self-renewal?

'Is the Brotherhood still infiltrated?' persisted Philippa.

'We don't know.' Ibrahim looked at his watch. 'We shall land in half an hour. You will become a brother, Hugo.'

'And what about me?' asked Philippa. 'Is there a Sisterhood?'

Ibrahim smiled. 'I'm afraid not. Men, as you know, have high status in my country.'

'So I'm to be on the sidelines. Hiding behind my veil.'

'You are a principal player.'

'It's no good,' said Hugo, with a rather desperate attempt at humour. 'You'll just have to get used to being a second-class citizen.'

Philippa stuck out her tongue at him and the sudden lightening of mood seemed to discomfort Ibrahim far more than their relentless questioning. 'I suggest you get some rest,' he said, with a flash of unsettling irritation. 'You will find the next few hours taxing.'

'There's something else,' she said.

'Well?'

'I was wondering. I know the Atlanteans can't leave the earth but can they leave the pyramid?'

'I believe they do so occasionally. They have manufactured various – receptacles. The casket, the globes, the disc.'

'Disc?'

'It's like an aircraft. A winged disc. The gods use the disc to observe the outside world and its follies. Just one more UFO.' He smiled slightly. 'Now I must close my eyes for a while – we shall be landing soon.'

The plane was met by three black Mercedes which drove across the Tarmac towards them as the aircraft engines were cut. They glided slowly and powerfully along the runway, their coachwork shining in the afternoon sun.

'They've got that funereal feel,' said Hugo, pausing at the top of the steps.

'I think they're meant to be reassuring,' Philippa replied, as they began to walk slowly down the steps with Ibrahim behind them.

The chauffeur of the second Mercedes was standing beside the open rear passenger door. The windows were of darkened glass and the sombre analogy of death was enhanced as they clambered inside into the cool, coffin-like interior with its aroma of expensive leather.

'The journey will take us an hour,' said Ibrahim as he settled back into the leather upholstery. 'Shall we have a Scotch?'

'I thought devout Muslims didn't drink,' Philippa reproved.

'This one does,' he said reaching for the discreet cabinet.

The three Mercedes nudged their way through the slow-moving city traffic and the entrepreneurial chaos of the Cairo streets. They sat in silence, sipping their whisky, conscious that their driver was not only talking into a phone but was always glancing into his wing mirror and up at the rooftops above them. Beside him, on the passenger seat, lay an automatic pistol and a Kalashnikov rifle.

A helicopter chattered out of the cobalt sky and dipped its way downwards. It levelled out about sixty feet above them, and Hugo saw the pilot giving their driver a thumbs-up sign which he returned. As they inched slowly past a bazaar Hugo asked:

'Why *are* we travelling by car? Wouldn't the helicopter be quicker and safer?'

'Quicker certainly, but we're safer here – part of the ant heap.'

Safer, thought Hugo doubtfully as the convoy came to a grinding halt, hemmed in by a truckload of squealing pigs and a small van that was piled high with furniture. Further back, under the dark awnings of the bazaar, he had the sensation of being watched as a beggar lurched up to the smoked glass of the car window, chipped enamel cup waving, eyes imploring. Chickens ran round him clucking wildly. Could he be blind? There was foam at the corners of his mouth. An epileptic? A madman? He was like a predatory animal, hovering menacingly. There must be hundreds of others out there, full of hunger and misery, reeking of death. Why couldn't the Atlanteans solve poverty, Hugo thought savagely, instead of sheltering in a pyramid.

Then he saw the boy standing on the edge of the crowd near a stall that was selling meat, staring directly into the car. Hugo felt a chill of premonition. Surely there was a strong similarity between him and the other boys – or were they all the same boy, he thought frantically. First he'd shot him in the Belfast hotel room, then he'd lured him into a trap in the Kuwaiti border town and now – here he was again. But how could they all be the same, reasoned Hugo, and as he stared the face seemed to change, and when the boy began to walk towards the stationary Mercedes, Hugo could see that he was smiling engagingly.

'Don't let him in,' hissed Philippa.

The smile widened as he fumbled at the door handle.

'For God's sake – '

The car moved sluggishly away, leaving the boy standing there, a begging opportunity missed, his features now clearly unfamiliar. Just a face in the crowd.

'No one can get in,' Ibrahim reassured him. 'There's a central locking system.'

Philippa squeezed Hugo's wrist. 'What was going on?'

But he simply shook his head wearily.

The convoy drove on, picking up speed, away from the centre of the town, through grey, dust-washed shanty suburbs. Then, without any warning, a goat ran across the path of the first Mercedes. The car struck the animal a glancing blow, knocking it into the rubble-strewn gutter. It lay there, blood at its mouth, the owner raising an angry fist as the car sped past.

Hugo turned to Ibrahim angrily. 'Couldn't he have avoided that?'

'We're in a hurry.'

'He didn't have to be barbaric.'

'We daren't stop. Better the goat than us.'

Now they were out of the network of streets the cars picked up even more speed, lurching over potholes, whilst animals and even human beings avoided them more by luck than judgement.

Eventually they drove out on to a broad highway with factories and warehouses on either side, and soon they were cruising at a hundred kilometres an hour until the factories slowly petered out and they entered a residential quarter. Large houses stood in their own grounds, with palm trees, swimming pools and gardens that were set back behind fencing and iron gates from which security lights and cameras hung. One set of gates was open and they caught a glimpse of a couple of large cars being lovingly polished by chauffeurs.

'The place to be,' commented Ibrahim, and Hugo looked at him sharply. Despite what he told us, he thought, we know nothing about him as a man.

'Are you married?' asked Philippa, clearly thinking along the same lines.

'Yes. I have a wife and two girls. I would like to spend more time with them. Soon, however, I will be able to. Hopefully.'

'When the gods have flown?'

'As you say.'

[137]

The cars turned off the road and were now proceeding at a brisk pace up a long and spacious drive that was lined by densely packed Cypress trees. Through them, Hugo could just make out landscaped gardens and a large swimming pool.

'A little ostentatious for a secret society,' commented Hugo.

'We hide behind our ostentation. As well as the sign I believe you missed at the front gate.'

'Which was?'

'Egyptian Trade Delegation.'

'Ah.'

'And, of course, the delegation functions. It's not just a front. We exist behind its halls of bureaucracy.'

The halls of bureaucracy turned out to be an exceedingly beautiful country house built in Colonial style, with a colonnaded façade and dormer windows protruding from the fourth floor. The walls were painted a dazzling white and a number of Rolls-Royces and Bentleys were parked under awnings outside. Each window had its own blinds and a canopy stretched from the central porticoed door.

The garden was formal in the French manner, with box hedges, gravel paths and flowers in tubs but not in borders. The paths led to a fountain where two cherubs upheld a huge stone cup with carvings of stallions and a jet of water that arched up into the sky and sprayed the wide, shallow basin below, draining away into a sloping duct. The spray from this shimmering golden fan, shot with translucent sunbeams, masked the summerhouse which was to the left of the fountain, nestling in a grassy hollow, overlooking the city below.

Six old men, all in Arab robes, sat cross-legged around a low table on which was a coffee pot and cups.

Ibrahim stood to one side.

As Hugo and Philippa entered, they were absorbed into a great stillness; no one moved or even looked up at them and only the splashing of the fountain broke the silence.

'Mr Fitzroy? Miss Neville?' He was emaciated, with stick-like wrists, the hands twisted and misshapen by arthritis.

'This is the Magus – Jamal Rashman, president of the Brother-hood of the Winged Disc.'

There was something rather chilling about him, Hugo decided, but at first he could not think why. He glanced at Philippa and saw that she was staring intently at the old man's gaunt profile, rather as if she was trying to satisfy herself about something. Then Jamal turned towards him and Hugo saw that he had no eyes; webbed skin, soft and pale, covered the sockets.

'There have been betrayals – we no longer trust each other,' Jamal intoned.

Ibrahim sat down and gestured to Hugo and Philippa to do the same.

'As a result the secret has been whispered abroad. The Iraqis lied to the gods. They told them that they could discover the day and time of the opening of the portal – the change in the earth's frequency that they have been awaiting so long. They told them there would be no emissaries – that the reincarnates would never come.' Jamal paused, his voice weak, the words difficult to make out. 'The gods initiated the rebirth of Islam; now they are exhausted and must leave to renew their strength. They will still watch over us but they must be persuaded that the Iraqi solution is not their means of escape.'

'Do the Iraqis have any chance of establishing the frequency change?' asked Hugo.

'No.' Jamal's voice was stronger, more anxious now. 'They cannot penetrate the Chamber of Records. It only exists in a spiritual dimension. But the Iraqis would do anything, say anything, to convince the gods that they will be their saviours.'

Jamal rose to his feet, and Hugo felt that this must be one of the most significant moments in the old man's life. He had waited so long for the hope they were bringing him, and it was clear he was terrified they might not be ready for the task – or even capable of fulfilling it.

'You must be spiritually strong,' he said. 'There is nothing physical in this attempt to release them. You must use all your powers – you must bring them together to unite your strength. Above all, you must prepare. If you fail, the Iraqis will persuade the gods to give them the formula for the poison, and if they do that – then there will be a holocaust. I can assure you – both of you – that the world could never recover from that. Only continuous war could result.' Jamal's sightless eyes were fixed on them, and they both knew that he was looking into their minds. Then he said, 'Let me show you what the poison – the terrible vapour – can do to human beings.'

The other members of the Brotherhood remained behind with Ibrahim as Jamal led Hugo and Philippa unerringly out of the summerhouse into the heat of the formal garden and then through palm trees towards another small building, its white stone shadowed. His blindness was no handicap, and he hardly hesitated as he opened the door of a viewing theatre with a small screen and a couple of rows of armchairs. He asked them to sit and then continued to explain.

'The gods have already given the Iraqis a mild formula of the gas which has been used on the Marsh Arabs. You will find what you see deeply disturbing. The cassette was sent to me as a warning.'

With only a slight hesitation, Jamal pressed a switch on the wall, the lights dimmed and images began to flicker on the screen.

The village was in a delta, a confluence of a number of different small rivers that had joined in marsh and estuary. The reed huts were scattered on a small promontory.

A dozen Arabs, mostly men and boys, scattered as Iraqi bombers swept low; some hid behind the dykes, whilst others threw themselves into a small wooden fishing vessel. The camera was at first unsteady as the planes flew low, belching out what looked like dense white smoke, some of which settled on the boat. Its occupants tried to cast off and then abandoned the task as the vapour intensified; their hands went to their eyes, their screams thickened in their throats. At first, Hugo thought that this was due to the bad video sound-recorder on the camera, but then he realized that the dreadful sound was for real.

The smoke cleared slightly to reveal the most appalling sight that even Hugo had ever seen in any war arena, and he choked back the nausea as Philippa clutched at the armrests of her chair. Transfixed with horror, he saw the features of the Marsh Arabs gradually dissolve, the skin burning, the eyes bulging and then imploding, blood streaming, hair falling away, the agony impossible to watch any longer. As they both turned away, Jamal stopped the video, but one image remained: the close-up of a child's ravaged, ruined face. Then the screen went dark.

Philippa rocked herself silently to and fro and Hugo could not bring himself to speak.

'We don't know the chemical make-up of the gas,' said Jamal. 'We'll probably never know.'

'And the Iraqis can process it?' demanded Hugo at last.

'No. They were given a small supply, fully prepared. By the gods.'

'Some gods,' muttered Philippa. 'Some fucking gods. Anyone who is prepared to concoct stuff like that can't be anything but demonic.'

'They are above such considerations,' replied Jamal. 'They are not beings of conscience or morality. They have the knowledge: their power is our eternal challenge.'

'A force that can be used for good or evil,' said Hugo angrily. 'How can you have respect for that?'

'Like Islam at its purest, there is much good; at its worst, wholly evil. The choice lies with us.'

'How can that stuff – that gas – be anything else but satanic?'

'I must assure you that it could be of great benefit to third world countries.'

'In what way?' asked Hugo, beside himself with rage. In his mind he could still see what had been the child's face.

'With a slight alteration in the compound, the gas can be used as a supremely productive fertilizer.'

There was a long silence.

'Who told you this?' said Hugo at last.

'The gods.'

'You are in contact with them?' asked Hugo.

'Of course. My mind is always open – tuned to receive communications from them at any time.'

'Don't the Atlanteans – your gods have *any* sense of responsibility?' persisted Philippa, outraged by his complacency. 'Surely they must know – must see that we are fallible and often make the wrong choice? How can they let thousands suffer for the decision of a few?' She glared at him, awaiting the predictable reply.

'They don't see things as we do,' replied Jamal unanswerably. 'Now – we are going to give you both a short time in which to prepare yourselves. Please do all you can to increase your spiritual strength.'

Jamal led them into a small meeting-room next door and then went away. They looked round in silence. Apart from a few cushions on the deep pile carpet and hessian hangings on the windowless walls, the room was unfurnished.

'We should make love,' said Philippa. 'It's the only way we can increase our strength.'

'Yes. I know that's true.'

'Can you do it – now?'

'I want to,' Hugo said. 'I want to go inside you – I want to be with you. You've reached out to me so much. I need to do the same to you – for you.'

'Do you love me?'

'More than I can say.'

'Show me.'

As they took off their clothes, they could hear Jamal praying in another room. His voice was distinct but unobtrusive, an accompaniment to their love-making. She *is* all spirit, thought Hugo. She never lost what we set out with when we commissioned the pyramid. But I did; gradually, over the lives I had, every ounce of spirit drained away until I was a burnt-out shell, living on evasion, sensation, indulgence. It's only now, at last, that I've come to understand: it's the spirit of self-sacrifice that is life.

Their love-making was tender and uplifting, and as they came to the climax they could hear Jamal quoting in English from the Koran:

'One is cast down to the earth, and one
Is lifted on high like the glorious sun.
Blessed is he who has wit to learn
How the favour of fortune may change and turn,
Whose head is not raised in his high estate,
Nor his heart in misfortune made desolate.'

When it was over, they lay naked side by side, holding hands, intensely aware of their unity of purpose.

'Do you feel strong?' she asked.

'Yes.'

'You won't be running away?'

'Not again. Never again.'

'Even if we have to be apart?'

'In this life?' he asked.

'In any life.'

'I love you, Philippa.'

'But do you love me enough to be alone?'

'Yes.'

'Are you sure?'

'I don't want to be away from you. Why do you – '

She rolled over on top of him and pushed his shoulders to the floor. 'I'm giving you myself, Hugo.'

The three Mercedes drove out into the desert in the same formation as before. The drive was long, but Hugo had never felt so confident, never felt so much himself; not the old Hugo that he had assumed was all he had, but the new Hugo, purposefully committed. He concentrated on the desert landscape of flawless sand-dunes, the occasional dried-up river beds, elemental boulders that looked as if they had been spat out from deep inside the interior of the earth, and camels on a skyline sharply etched in the hard light.

Jamal sat opposite them, his webbed sockets mercifully dimmed by the shadowy light, while Ibrahim sprawled in the corner, his eyes closed, possibly asleep but more probably listening to whatever they might say.

[143]

'I'm afraid,' Philippa whispered.

'So am I. But we have the strength – we must use it.'

'I feel we've been waiting for this – like Jamal – for ever. Once we're there at the pyramid – ' She paused, not wanting to continue.

'We've fulfilled our destiny?'

'Yes. Does it mean we're going to die? Like insects at the end of their cycle? Is that what's going to happen?'

'I don't know.' Hugo could bring no comfort. 'We're together still. We'll always be together.' But then he remembered what she had said while they were making love: Do you love me enough to be alone?

The convoy sped on down the highway and gradually Hugo felt a darkness coming over him and saw himself as a moth hovering over a flame. Night was falling over the desert and shadows covered the sand as the sun set in a blazing halo. He imagined primeval beings stirring in the dunes, waking after a thousand years of sleep. Hugo saw himself and Philippa walking across the desert, eternal travellers, slowly nearing the pyramid, its mouth open, a crouched animal, waiting to receive them into eternal darkness. So often had he been at the point of death, so often had fate seized him, snatching him away, preserving him for this moment. Then the winged serpents took him.

'Hugo.'

'Yes?'

'You were asleep. We're here now. We're at the pyramid.' But it was not Philippa's voice.

He opened his eyes to see nothing. The fear intensified. The serpents were inside him.

'Philippa.'

'It's me. Ibrahim.'

'Where is she?'

'Asleep too.'

Hugo reached out in the darkened interior of the Mercedes and slowly woke her.

'The pyramid,' she muttered.

[144]

'We'll be all right.' The fear twisted in Hugo's stomach like a live animal.

'Mr Fitzroy?' Jamal spoke gently. 'Are you prepared? I have been praying for you both.'

10

THE GODS IN THEIR CASKET

The Great Pyramid was majestic in the sharp moonlight. Built of weathered stone, it dominated the desert, its apex reaching up to the glinting brilliance of the stars.

Jamal paused and then urgently beckoned them on towards the other façade, where a small metal door was let into the stone. The terror in the pit of Hugo's stomach coiled, ready to spring. Jamal took out a key.

'Follow me.' He produced a powerful flashlight and, with rising trepidation, Hugo and Philippa followed him inside.

Jamal shone the powerful beam around the interior. The floor of the pyramid was sandy and bare and the walls rose around them claustrophobically. There was a musty, acrid, chemical smell, and as the flashlight continued to sweep, the interior seemed even smaller. Immediately Hugo noticed the same kind of glutinous liquid he had seen in the building in the desert. Some of it was also splashed on the walls.

'What *is* that strange liquid?' he asked. It was not something that Ibrahim had been able to explain.

'It's called Dacta – the gods nourish themselves and then excrete this substance. Part of its chemical make-up is used in the making of the vapour.' Jamal turned towards them, his face in shadow behind the flashlight. 'That is their physical nature. It's not a great deal. The rest is pure spirit.'

'They leave the pyramid, then?' asked Philippa.

'The Disc will take them out into the desert where they synthesize Dacta from desert plants.'

'They must have gone into the Iraqi monitoring station that we stopped at.'

'Yes – they regularly visited the place. They were deeply concerned they were under surveillance but the Iraqis claimed it was for their protection. I don't think they were satisfied.'

'You say "the Iraqis".' Hugo was impatient. 'Just how many know about this – or *think* they know?'

'Saddam Hussein – and a few of his most trusted advisers. No more.'

'And he believes?'

'Yes.'

'He's been here? Seen the Atlanteans – communicated with them?'

'He has not done this personally. But a member of his cabinet has.'

'This person came to the pyramid with you?'

'I had no choice in the matter. If I die – a trusted negotiator is lost.'

'And Hussein believes? Believes when thousands wouldn't?' Philippa was incredulous – and suspicious.

'He believes. His advisor has been monitoring the situation for many months now. And you have seen the video.' The old man's voice trembled slightly. 'What more does he need? What more do *you* need?'

'We need to *see*,' replied Hugo.

Jamal gave his flashlight to Philippa, walked slowly to a hollow in the wall and fumbled inside. Eventually he drew out a metal casket which flashed acid green in the beam.

'Please do not illuminate the interior.'

Jamal slid away the lid of the casket and, rather like opening a child's pencil-box, slowly revealed what was inside. Hugo's first thought was that it was dried skin. Then he realized they were winged serpents. Jamal placed the casket reverently on the floor and crouched down beside it. One of the things had decomposed and was simply a mass of what looked like pale fronds. Hugo had never felt so afraid in his life; he was confronting a miracle – and the miracle was his responsibility. Yes – Philippa's, too, but he knew intuitively that she had given him her spiritual strength and now it was up to him to reach out to Brent and find out what Thoth wanted him to do. That was his role, and he felt a blinding terror of where he would have to go. For if the present existence of the gods was a miracle then he would have to provide another one to assure their release. What had Turgenev said? The words flooded into his mind: 'Whatever a man prays for, he prays for a miracle. Every prayer reduces itself to this. "Great God, grant that twice two be not four."'

'The gods are resting,' said Jamal reverently. 'Be patient.' He squatted down beside them, his webbed sockets wrinkled, as if he was somehow seeing underneath their pale folds. A glow of moonlight washed the sandy floor of the pyramid and when Hugo looked up he could see the closed portal. Twice two equals four? He would have to be better than that.

The serpents had not moved, but when he glanced across at Philippa he saw she looked entranced.

'Do you see something?'

'Be patient.' But it was not Philippa's voice that replied.

'What are you seeing?'

Her face was radiant, but she made no reply.

'Stop resisting, Hugo,' whispered Jamal.

'I can't help it.' He felt like a child left out of a game, and a wave of panic swept him.

'Take my hand,' said Philippa.

He reached out and her flesh was as cold as stone in the desert at night. When he looked at it in the hard light, he could see a web of tiny veins. Then he saw bone.

'Don't be afraid. We've been together a long time, Hugo. Do you remember those days? When we watched them building this pyramid?'

Hugo's head spun. Now the serpents – the Atlanteans – the

[148]

gods – were floating in gossamer globes above him, and when he looked back into the casket there was nothing there but dust. The pyramid was now a vast cathedral-like space, scented with balsam and sandalwood. Soft light bathed the interior, the floor was polished stone and the walls gleamed black and lustrous.

'Dad.'

Brent was walking towards him from behind a sandcastle. The tide roared, but it was retreating and the castle walls were no longer threatened.

'Dad.'

He was covered in wet sand and clasping a spade. Then he was a little older, springing up to the cliff top to greet him. 'I've got something to show you.'

'What is it?'

'A secret.'

'Can Philippa come?'

'Where's Mum?'

'At home. Can Philippa come with us?'

'All right.'

Hugo and Philippa stood hand in hand, waiting for Brent to show them his secret.

They were walking through grey darkness along a wood-panelled corridor. There was another smell now. Ink and sweat and gym shoes. School? Impossible.

'Do you remember Marlborough, Dad? You should. It was you who sent me here.'

Philippa clutched Hugo's hand. This time her grip was warm. He saw a huge dining-hall where dozens of boys in dark clothes were eating. On a rostrum he saw men in gowns. Above them floated the gossamer globes. Sound came and went like the waves on the beach of Tiderace. The clatter of cutlery, the buzz of conversation and the relentless chant of derision, 'Fitzroy wets his bed. Fitzroy wets his bed.'

'I was bullied, Dad.'

'Where are we going?' Hugo could hardly bring out the words

[149]

from the deadly chill of the pit inside him, but Philippa's grip grew tighter.

'The Chamber of Records.'

Brent sounded careless, almost matter-of-fact, and Hugo could now see that he was wearing the same dark clothes as the other boys.

'*Here?*'

'I was trapped here, Dad. I couldn't get out – Thoth was trapped – just like the gods. Now it's right for us all to go, but only you can find the right time.'

'Why me?'

'Because you're powerful. You've been given strength. Come on, Dad.'

'Here?' Hugo asked. 'Why here?'

They were standing outside a battered wooden door marked LIBRARY.

'This used to be my hidey-hole – away from the bullies.'

'And this is the Chamber of Records?' Philippa's voice was distant and incredulous.

'Yes.'

Brent opened the door and Hugo saw the beam penetrating the high mullioned windows. Polished tables, book-lined shelves, magazines in a rack, newspapers in a pile, battalions of radiators, warmth and comfort. It was safe in here; Hugo knew that no harm could befall them because this was Brent's sanctuary. He looked up to see a glass-domed skylight. The portal. His son was standing in the beam now, the glow turning him golden, giving him flaxen hair and the look of a young god, of Thoth himself.

'Here it is,' said Brent. The beam ended on a pile of books, surmounted by the Koran. As Philippa lifted it up, her hands trembled. Below was a slim volume. Macbeth, by William Shakespeare.

*

'When I read that here, Dad, I knew that this had nothing to do with me, that I was different. Eventually the reason became clear: I was Thoth.' Brent's voice was adult now. 'Pick it up,' he said authoritatively.

Slowly Hugo complied.

'Keep it in the beam.'

Again he did as he was told. A page fell open, illuminated by strong, revealing light.

> She should have died hereafter;
> There would have been a time for such a word.
> Tomorrow, and tomorrow, and tomorrow,
> Creeps in this petty pace from day to day.
> To the last syllable of recorded time;
> And all our yesterdays have lighted fools
> The way to dusty death. Out, out brief candle.
> Life's but a shadow, a poor player
> That struts and frets his hour upon the stage.
> And then is heard no more; it is a tale
> Told by an idiot, full of sound and fury,
> Signifying nothing.

Hugo noticed a slip of paper stuck in the margin of the book. As he unfolded it, he saw the writing was Brent's.

'The other lines – they're from Henry Vaughan. They came into my head when I saw the globes.'

'*You* saw them,' Philippa whispered.

'Oh yes. I was sitting here in my hideaway when they drifted in with the sunbeam to tell me who I was. I could see the disc, hovering outside the window.' He spoke with a boyish enthusiasm.

'And who *we* were?' asked Philippa urgently.

'I didn't know that for a long time,' replied Brent hesitantly.

Hugo read the words aloud.

> Oh how I long to travel back,
> And tread again that ancient track
> That I might once more reach that plain,

[151]

Where first I left my glorious train;
        From when th'enlightened spirit sees
        That shady city of palm trees.

At the bottom of the lines was a scrawled note: 'At 7.03 a.m. Sept 18.'

'That's the day after tomorrow,' said Philippa.

'And there will be no other chance – not for another 25,000 years. They've hung on with the promise of the light, but already one of them has gone to dust – '

Brent grinned his schoolboy grin. Hugo saw that there was ink on his cheek and one of his fingernails was broken. He longed to throw his arms around him.

'Go on,' urged Philippa.

'I'm flesh and blood, Dad,' grinned the schoolboy and Hugo embraced him. As he did so, he felt a surge of power and authority – the strength he had taken away from his son by running for cover had joined the strength he had received from Philippa in their love-making. How empty he had been.

Brent drew away from him and then flung his arms around Philippa.

'What are we to do now?' she asked urgently.

'There is very little time. You must go to Nazra and then return to the pyramid – well before the hour of the change in frequency. If you aren't there, the gods cannot leave. There'll be no power.'

'Nazra? Where's Nazra? Why do we have to go there? Can't we just wait here – with you – until the time comes?'

But already Brent was walking out of the library and through the crowded dining-hall. The meal was over and boys and masters were standing, singing to the accompaniment of a piano. Abruptly the hymn stopped and a young priest stepped on to the rostrum.

'To the roof that rises over us we submit this prayer: that the gods choose to show us the path of righteousness – and not the descent into the pit. The price of this evil is too great to pay for freedom.'

Then they were alone, hurrying down the panelled corridors, their feet making no sound, the space growing large, the walls

[152]

becoming those of the pyramid. The roof soared – and they sat down beside Jamal and the empty casket.

'Have you been successful?'

'Yes,' said Philippa.

'Now sleep.'

'We can't sleep,' said Hugo, but exhaustion swept over him. 'Where is Basra? We've got to go there. Now.'

'You will learn about Nazra – but only in sleep.' Jamal's voice had a complete finality to it, and almost immediately Hugo began to battle against a drowsiness that became increasingly persistent.

He was flying low across the dunes, the wind howling in his ears, taking him on what felt like a hard, buoyant shoulder of rushing air. It was still dark but a crescent moon revolved, a splinter of light that illuminated the twisting, soaring path. Several times he saw dried-out river beds below him, and in one the word BASRA heaved and pulsated, as if each stroke was made of serpents. Suddenly the lettering began to unwind and he saw the serpents sliding towards the dunes, racing him and the wind in fast, slithering, sinewy movement. Then he saw the cluster of buildings, low, one-storey, huddled round a small oasis fringed by desiccated palm trees. Even in the darkness, Nazra had a burnt-out feel, continually savaged by blazing sun, cool now, but blistered. The dunes rose away to the west. Built into one of them was an exact replica of the compound they had discovered on the road in Iraq, but as he stared down at it the wind took him high over the top and then he was falling, spiralling down towards its interior and the serpents that were now coiled below. Struggling in their midst, their bodies split and their bellies opened as long dark tunnels. At the end of each was a video screen holding the pyramid's image. As he crawled towards it, the screen darkened and he saw the gods in their spheres. Inside his mind the question was insistent, imploring, yearning.

When?

'Sunrise. Tomorrow. At 7.03.'

You have no time.

'For what?'

To destroy the vapour.

'The gas? *You* must do that.'

We cannot. They have the formula.

'*All of it?*'

Yes.

'Why can't you use your powers? Don't you realize what the gas can do?'

The choice is theirs. The voice in his mind was very faint now.

'Where are you going?'

Beyond the stars.

'To do what?'

To build.

'Atlantis?'

But there was no reply and the end of the serpent was a wall of black flesh that was fast approaching him.

'The sun's coming up,' Philippa whispered. The wall became her face, and through the cracks around the portal Hugo saw light. For a few moments he felt bewildered, as if he should be remembering something that kept elusively slipping away. Then the beam appeared with such force and suddenness that his heart began pounding so heavily he wondered if he was having a coronary.

Philippa stepped into the beam, and for a moment Hugo was afraid. Then he joined her. They held hands, travelling up the beam until they were near the apex of the pyramid, from which they could see vast tracts of empty rolling desert.

'It's moving,' Philippa said. 'The earth's moving.'

Still they rose, until they had left the pyramid far below and were overlooking the lip of the world – a world of shifting sand fast becoming ocean – an ocean that boiled and heaved in great dark crests. The beam pierced the waves and an island rose from the tumult. Slowly, Hugo recognized the tiny land mass as Tiderace. Again the pyramid appeared on the cliff top. Walking towards it were three naked figures: Thoth and Hermes and Isis

– the beginning of the reincarnations that would lead to the end of the Atlanteans' time on earth.

The beam had disappeared and the interior of the pyramid was dark, cold and desolate. Even Jamal seemed to have left them.

'It happened,' Philippa murmured. 'It *did* happen, Hugo.'

'Wait.' Hugo was staring up into the darkness. 'What's this? Another beam?'

The gossamer globe hovered some twelve feet above them but it was impossible to see the interior. Nevertheless, for the first time, Hugo could feel *their* fear, could sense the doubts of the creatures above.

'I've told you when the portal will open,' said Hugo. 'And I'm going to Basra. But I don't know how to destroy the vapour.'

We need your strength, said the increasingly familiar voice in his mind.

'Strength? I'm weak. You are the gods.'

There is great danger.

'What should we do?' asked Hugo.

Go to Nazra now. Both of you.

'I still don't know what the hell I'm meant to do when I get there.'

He will be waiting.

'Who?'

The globe was rising, the telepathy becoming fainter.

'Will *you* give us strength?' demanded Philippa.

But there was no response.

Hugo turned to Philippa in dismay as the iron door rasped open and Ibrahim appeared, looking as benign and as calm as ever.

'You have established the time?' he asked deferentially.

'Sunrise. Tomorrow. At 7.03.'

'Thank you.'

There is something different about him, thought Hugo. Something barely discernible. Instinctively he knew that Philippa felt the same.

'I've got something for you.' Ibrahim reached into the pocket of his jacket and then rammed the small automatic weapon into Philippa's stomach. Hugo watched unbelievingly, unconvinced that this could possibly be happening. Soon, in a few seconds time, he would be telling them both that it was all a joke, a test, a mistake, a reminder, a frightener. That was it. He was only trying to put the wind up them, to bring them back under his control.

'Who are you?' Philippa whispered.

'Tarik Ibrahim.' He smiled at her in genuine amusement. 'Working for Iraqi Intelligence. I thought that would surprise you – just when you were beginning to trust me. I'm afraid I've been a man of many parts. But you have plumbed the depths and reached the last. The real me. The real loyalty.'

Hugo, was numb now, as if he had suddenly been anaesthetized, but Philippa seemed composed. 'The Brotherhood – the old men in the summerhouse?'

'We are *all* loyal to Iraq and to Saddam Hussein. The original Brotherhood were executed some months ago.'

'And Jamal?'

'He is loyal to Saddam as well.'

'So everything was a charade.'

'We wanted to know how genuine you were. Now we understand that you *are* probably capable of releasing the gods, and that is, of course, totally out of the question.'

Hugo at last found himself able to speak. 'You're going to execute us too?' Yet he still found the situation unreal; he was waiting for the spell to break, for Ibrahim to give them both a good reason for his melodrama.

Ibrahim ignored him, continuing to address Philippa. 'You must accept that your role is over. Our chemists have analysed the sample they gave us and will be manufacturing it at Nazra. The Atlanteans will not be allowed to leave but we shall convince them that they can providing they give us the additional chemical ingredients that can produce a more toxic gas.'

'I would have thought the one you had was already lethal enough,' Philippa replied.

'And the Egyptians permit you to manufacture it here in their own country?' asked Hugo incredulously, the numbness leaving him and the grim reality of the situation returning. They had been used – and were now to be discarded.

'Under the guise of a germ-warfare research station ostensibly owned by the Egyptian government. Our nations have common enemies. You must surely realize that.' Ibrahim was as courteous and as benign as ever. 'No one will know from where the gas emanates. And you have already seen how fast-acting it is. We shall destroy thousands.'

'Are both governments *really* aware of what you're doing?' Philippa was still calm, but Hugo felt the cold rage rising inside her. There must be some way of disarming Ibrahim without a fatality.

'Some key members. Yes.'

'In other words – only the fanatics.'

'That is not the way I would put it,' he said dismissively. 'You are of little significance now but we can't afford to take any risks. And there's another problem, isn't there, Miss Neville? You are carrying a child – an Atlantean – and he could be a great danger to us.'

'Where's the casket?' asked Hugo, trying to distract him.

'In its sanctuary.' Ibrahim didn't look round.

'And the gods are unharmed?'

'Oh, we shan't harm them. Who knows what use they could still be put to? Eventually they'll lose power and wither away, but that thing inside you won't, will it?'

Ibrahim shot Philippa in the stomach and went on firing. Hugo was stunned by the sudden horror of it all, watching her stagger, clasping her body protectively, perhaps as numbed as he was. But Ibrahim had done it casually, almost kindly, and Hugo saw that he was still smiling politely as he went on pumping bullets into her.

Philippa took a step towards the casket, her eyes glazing over and the blood pouring from the holes in her body. Then, slowly, she

[157]

began to fall. Transfixed, Hugo watched her crumple on to the floor. He had lost her. He had lost her in a few seconds. Where was the gods' protection now? He thought of the ignition keys in the truck, the diesel, the water, the – if they could guide them as well as that, how could this unbelievable tragedy have occurred?

Philippa writhed, rolling over a couple of times, her hands clutching at her stomach, trying to stem the flow. Her eyes rolled up and she tried to say something, but only a bubbling sound emerged, her mouth opening again and again.

A small globe rose from the blood below her waist and soared gently to the top of the pyramid. Unlike the other globes that were cloudy, this one was clear, and rather than a serpent Hugo saw a baby, lying on its back, gurgling slightly, kicking its legs in happy abandon. Ibrahim fired and fired again at the globe, but it was so high now, so indistinct, that it made an impossible target.

Hugo flung himself down beside Philippa, yelling, shouting, screaming, compelling her to live, demanding that the gods, with all their powers, return her to him.

The trigger of the pistol clicked uselessly, and consumed with manic rage Hugo flung himself at Ibrahim and they fell to the sandy floor, rolling, thrashing, yelling, snarling, locked together like animals. As they continued to roll, Ibrahim lost his grip on the gun and Hugo was able to sweep it away, but immediately Ibrahim was astride him, screaming abuse, no longer gentle or benign or anonymous, showing his passion at last, pressing his fingers into Hugo's eyes. The intensity of the pain gave him enough desperate strength to kick him off, and soon they were struggling in Philippa's blood. He could glimpse her, still alive, her eyes staring up at the almost invisible globe, her lips moving slightly, making the bubbling sounds that were so appalling to hear. For a fraction of a second, he felt Ibrahim weaken and was on top of him immediately, grinding his knees into his shoulders and crashing his head again and again on the floor. Eventually, after what seemed a very long time, he was still. Gasping for breath, Hugo got up and knelt down by Philippa's side.

'I'm not going very far, Hugo. Only to another room. I'll be close by.' Her voice was clear and purposeful, but she did not speak again and when he checked her pulse it was faint. Blood

[158]

was coming from her mouth now, a thick red stream, and then great gobbets of a darker substance. Her eyes were open, staring into his own, and for a moment he thought he saw a flicker of recognition. Her lips were moving again but when she spoke it was Brent's voice. 'Go to Nazra. Drive south.' The lips stopped moving, a little more blood came – and then the flow ceased. She was an empty shell.

Hugo kissed her fingers and then her cheek. Philippa was still very warm. He stood up, glanced down at Ibrahim and then moved cautiously towards the door of the pyramid. Why should he go to Nazra? Would she, in some miraculous way, be waiting for him there? His hopes soared, sustaining him as Hugo realized his long journey was not over yet. Perhaps the gods were still guiding their destinies. Perhaps they would restore Philippa to him.

11

BIRTHRIGHT

Hugo ran out into the blinding white light of the desert; immediately the heat descended on him like a suffocating blanket and he could feel it bearing down on him. Jamal was sitting in the sand dunes with a couple of younger men, talking, brewing up coffee. They looked prosaic and mundane in this world of gods and birth and sudden death. None of them looked up and Hugo wondered if the ignition key was in Ibrahim's jeep or whether it was in one of his pockets. Surely he couldn't expect any more miracles now.

Not wanting to risk alerting Jamal and his companions, Hugo darted back into the pyramid where he was immediately enveloped by its stillness. Philippa and Ibrahim lay on their backs. She had her eyes open and Hugo knelt down beside her to gently pull down the lids. He kissed her again and then began to search Ibrahim's pockets. Finally, to his relief, he found the keys. Catching sight of the discarded revolver he picked it up, wiped away the blood and shoved it in his pocket.

Hugo cautiously returned to the door, his mind reeling. She was dead. But would he see her again at Nazra? Was there any point in praying to the Atlanteans?

Before Jamal's companions could react, Hugo was in the jeep and had started the engine, seeing to his relief that there was a compass on the dashboard. Jamming his foot hard down on the accelerator he swung the vehicle in a wide arc, and sensing something had gone wrong, Jamal slowly rose to his feet while the others ran across the sand-hills to a Suzuki that was parked on the far side of the dirt road.

Knowing he had a good head start Hugo was determined to press home his advantage, gunning the accelerator, watching the speedometer rise. The dirt road wound on before him, and the wind that had been light became hot and blasting, lashing the sand so that he could only just see. His eyes smarting and stinging, he tried to look back. There was no sign of pursuit, but the hot wind was blowing so much sand across the road that he could not be sure. Tying a handkerchief around his mouth and nose and dragging on a pair of dark glasses he found on the passenger seat, Hugo stamped hard down on the accelerator again. Gradually he not only lost count of time but also of distance as his consciousness narrowed into a whirling reddish-brown funnel, and he had the sensation of being in the womb, about to see the strangely dysfunctional world outside. The roaring of the jeep's engine, the stingingly hot sand, the sensation of speed gradually faded, leaving him in a void with his grief.

'I'm only in the other room.' Philippa's voice caressed his ears. His mind raced, searching for hope. There came a strange, uneasy conviction: if the Brotherhood of the Winged Disc had all been eliminated by Iraqi security, then he was the last remaining brother. He was the protector of the gods – all they had left – and always would be, whatever life or form he had to take on. And if only he could be reunited with Philippa – and he prayed fervently to them that he would be – then he would serve them always, in whatever capacity they desired.

Gradually, the hot wind began to die and the visibility to improve, but glancing over his shoulder at the gradually clearing haze Hugo could still see no sign of pursuit and he drove on, watching the fuel gauge. It stood at just under half. Was this to be a re-run of the episode in the truck he had shared with Philippa? Was there fuel in Nazra, or perhaps another vehicle? Could he have been set up to run into another trap, to be stranded and to fail to give whatever remaining strength he had to the Atlanteans?

The flies came in the late afternoon and gathered around the jeep so that he could only just see the strip of road. They formed a dense black cloud but the phenomenon only affected him glancingly. He was now no longer sure where he was – or even what he was attempting to do; the appalling loss of Philippa dominated him. He had seen her die, but could their miracles replace her blown-away stomach? Would he find her waiting for him at Nazra? The thought beat in his head and became an insistent prayer.

The cloud of flies lifted and hovered above him, fanning out in the hot air, pin-pointing the way forward, but as he drove, Philippa totally dominated his thoughts. They had only been together, at least in this present life, for a few weeks and Hugo still felt he hardly knew her. Nevertheless, he loved her completely, achingly, all-embracingly. He could feel her spirituality, her mysticism – all the qualities he lacked – and realized that through knowing her he was changed, abandoning his pursuit of material success for the spiritual strength of self-sacrifice. He had come such a long way on his journey – from self-deceiving hedonist to a man stripped of all hypocrisy, standing on the edge of a mystical world of which she was already part. He had to plunge in after her. But how? The road to Basra was the only thing he could now see clearly. Was everything else to remain hidden? The gods? Their ultimate powers? His own? Philippa?

Two hours later, Hugo arrived at Nazra. The village was fronted by a small scummy-looking lake around which a few camels grazed. A boy was sitting in the shallows and a few yards away there was a group of dull white buildings that faced inwards, huddling away from the heat, turning their backs on the water that was their life-force. A few chickens scratched around in an outer ring of wire netting and there was an untidy heap of

[162]

derelict cars and trucks in a wide gully. A herd of verminous-looking goats lay on the hard beaten sand near the water and Hugo supposed the boy was their goatherd. A radio played somewhere amongst the houses and there was a strong stench of dung.

Hugo searched for signs of fuel and then, to his relief, saw a pump at the back of a run-down building that might just pass for a garage. He clambered back into the jeep and drove down towards the lake. It looked cool, inviting, and on impulse he jumped out and plunged in, slaking his thirst regardless of the filthy water.

The boy watched him lazily, his presence no surprise. He wore a bedouin head-dress, but the remainder of his clothing consisted only of grubby shorts and tee-shirt; there was something familiar in his chestnut eyes.

'Where are you from?'

Hugo stared at the boy disbelievingly. How could a goatherd speak English? Fluent English which bore no trace of a foreign accent. Then he realized the voice was his son's.

'I was waiting.'

'Who are you?'

'Al-Naratin.'

'*Who* are you?'

'That's who I am.'

'How come you speak such good English?' persisted Hugo.

'From you.'

'What the hell do you mean?'

'From you, sir.'

Hugo tried to speak but the words stuck in his throat. Then, with an enormous effort, he blurted out, 'Are you my son?'

'I am Al-Naratin,' the boy repeated impatiently.

'For God's sake – '

'I am here to take you to Christopher.' The boy seized Hugo's hand. 'Come.'

*

Nazra was built around a square, in the centre of which was a small mosque. Its minarets and cupola were crudely executed and the red-washed walls had faded to a dim ochre. A few bedouin sat in the shadows, more chickens scratched and scurried in the hard-packed earth and some caged birds sang mournfully in the shadowed arches. There was an atmosphere of timelessness about the place and its scarred plaster, dark alleys and sun-baked buildings made Hugo feel wary. He had been in places like this before. They were dangerous.

The boy tugged at his hand, and in the back of his mind he heard Brent's voice on Tiderace. 'Come on, Dad. Race you to the top.'

The interior of the mosque was dim and smelt of spice and aromatic herbs and unwashed human bodies. Slowly, Hugo made out the figure of a European who sat cross-legged on a prayer mat. When he saw Hugo, he rose reluctantly to his feet and came over to him, a slight frown on his face as if he was annoyed at being disturbed.

'Hugo Fitzroy?'

'Yes.' He was wary.

'I'm Christopher Denning.' He spoke with an American accent. 'I'm director of the laboratory here.' He hesitated as if he had an unpleasant duty to carry out.

'Who does it belong to?' asked Hugo assertively.

'The Egyptian government,' he replied drily.

'And the Iraqis?'

'I'm not with you,' he said, and shrugged irritably, as if he had been forced into the encounter and wished it would quickly end. 'I gather you were sent here by Jamal Rashid and that you wish to photograph our germ warfare experiments.'

Hugo thought fast and then asked, 'Am I allowed to do that?' He had a sudden instinct that Denning was playing a game – a game in which he was expected to know the moves.

'Our government is anxious the West should know we're doing all we can to counter Hussein's nerve gas. There is nothing secret

[164]

here now – we've completed the experiments.' He spoke quite loudly and his voice echoed in the darkened building.

'And were they successful?'

'I can't tell you that.'

'Will they continue?'

'We don't know.'

Hugo felt irresolute, knowing he was working so totally in the dark. He had no plan, but when had he ever had that luxury during his long journey? And he didn't know the rules of Denning's game.

'Are you an Egyptian citizen?'

'No, but I'm a Muslim convert.' Denning paused, as if making an unwelcome decision. 'Would you like to come and take a look at our work? Then you can decide what you want to photograph.'

'What about security?'

'It's been lifted. But we're expecting Mr Ibrahim. I gather you know him well, and of course it's through him that you received clearance.'

Hugo looked at him in some bewilderment and then saw movement at the back of the mosque. Were they being watched? Was that why Denning was looking at him so intensely?

They crossed the twilit square together, heading down an alley between two buildings that looked as if they were held together by a combination of impacted mud and wattle.

Hugo stole a covert glance at his new companion. He was small and dapper, despite the bedouin clothing which hung on him voluminously. Somewhere in his sixties, with a small grey beard, his neat, regular features had considerable sensitivity, but he was radiating tension and kept staring nervously into the shadows of the buildings. 'I'm going to stop off before we get to the lab.' Denning paused at a small stone house without a door.

'I don't have much time,' said Hugo impatiently.

'Surely you'd like something to drink after your arduous journey?' There was an unmistakable message in Denning's eyes. 'You really must be advised by me,' he added.

[165]

They walked up a flight of cool stairs and into a single box-like room that had a kitchen leading off it. The furnishings were sparse – a few cushions on the floor, a couple of texts and a shelf of books, largely devoted to Islam. Denning went into the kitchen and returned with a pitcher of cold water and two glasses.

Hugo drank and surreptitiously looked at his watch. Nearly seven. Only twelve hours to go. What the hell was he going to do? When would the situation become clear?

'Sit down.' The instruction was peremptory.

Dutifully Hugo did as he was told and sat amongst the cushions, leaning against the cool wall, looking out of the large window to the street below.

'I think it best to tell you as much as I know. Obviously there were security people in the mosque and I couldn't speak openly. I came here – but I've got to go fast. OK.'

'OK.' Hugo's nerves screamed. How long was this going to take?

'I know how much of a hurry you're in and I appreciate the urgency, but you also have to understand my credentials, so please don't interrupt – or think any of this information is irrelevant.' Denning paused and then began to talk very fast. 'A few months ago I had a spiritual experience – far more important to me than my conversion to Islam. I began to dream about a pyramid. So did my son.'

The adrenalin raced in Hugo's veins. Was Denning a friend or an enemy? He fingered the empty, useless gun, knowing that he had no protection but not really caring either way. She was dead. His life – their life – had ended. What did it matter if Denning turned out to be another Ibrahim?

'There were globes with winged serpents inside them,' he was explaining. 'Each night the dream repeated itself but never advanced, always concluding as a globe floated towards me. Then, finally, the visions were extended.'

'I don't understand – ' Hugo was becoming agitated.

'Please bear with me. We saw you in the globe – my son Garry and I.'

'Me?'

'And a woman and a boy. Then we saw you without the woman, on an island, but with the boy. Gradually, each night, your story unfolded. We saw you begin the journey, and we also saw other journeys you had made in other lives. We listened to your son read from his journal and we began to understand.'

Is this a trap, wondered Hugo. He couldn't possibly afford to run the risk of coming clean. 'I don't understand what you're talking about,' he said lamely.

'You *must* trust me, Mr Fitzroy,' said Denning with a spurt of anger. 'I *know* why you're here – and I know how little time we have. At 7.03. Sunrise, isn't it?'

Hugo froze.

'This is *not* some kind of trap,' Denning insisted.

'What is it then?'

'A solution. At least I can promise you that.'

'Go on.'

'I came here two years ago as a senior chemist in charge of an anti-germ-warfare programme. We wanted an antidote to some lethal gas Saddam Hussein was using against the Marsh Arabs. I was known as a convert to Muslim fundamentalism but I am also a leader in my scientific field so it wasn't long before I was approached by an Egyptian security officer who told me the Iraqis were making a new kind of nerve gas – and that the sample I was examining was far less potent than the level they were going to achieve. I was scared out of my mind because the sample I had already received was absolutely deadly. By now I was dream-watching your journey, understanding the Atlanteans' desperation, and gradually I began to realize that our spiritual journey was running parallel to yours and that I had a role to play in their release. I knew that my spell of duty was coming to an end and realized that I would be replaced by someone who might be prepared to reverse the role of our operation – to make the gas rather than to analyse the stuff. What's more, I now knew that the formula for the even more lethal variety was about to be released. I therefore decided to make it clear to my intelligence contact that I was an anti-Semite, a far more fanatical fundamentalist than they had expected. Over a period of weeks I was successful in convincing the joint Arab investors in this project that I was the man for the job. The first formula was bad enough, but when I assessed the second I realized that it would achieve carnage on a scale and of a description never seen before.'

I've got to trust him, thought Hugo, whatever the risks. But how had he managed to see so much, and who had inspired his visions? Could the Atlanteans have a moral code after all? Had they planted Denning as a longstop, or was he merely another member of the new Brotherhood? And, above all, who was this son whom he had shared his visions with? Were they light walkers too? The main point, however, was that time was running out and he knew that he could do nothing on his own.

'Have you had other experiences?' Hugo probed, determined to understand everything despite the deadline. He could almost see the sand in the hour-glass running out and could hardly contain his impatience.

'Yes. I remember seeing a car that was later to injure my sister, and I witnessed my mother's death in a plane accident some days before it happened. Somewhere in my mind I watched a tidal wave build up; two days later it hit the shore in Florida. I expect I had lots of smaller, less significant experiences, but those were the big ones. Until now.'

'So the Atlanteans are hedging their god-damn bets,' said Hugo bitterly. 'Guiding, manipulating, facilitating. But the bottom line is this: if we haven't got the strength to release them, they seem to think the Iraqis can.'

'Yes – they seem convinced that they can succeed if you fail, but that's the bit I know they've got wrong.' Denning was adamant. 'We both know the time of the change in frequency but we have our very special, separate roles – and strengths. You are the sole survivor of three light walkers, and you alone have the power to assist the change – to release them. But only I can destroy the gas.'

Hugo nodded. 'What *is* this formula?'

'You know I can't tell you that.'

'It was used before – in Atlantis? All those thousands of years ago?' He was incredulous.

'Yes.'

'There's something else – ' Hugo hesitated. 'Did you know that Philippa was pregnant when she died?'

'I'm sorry – '

'Impregnated by the gods. And *when* she died, her child – the thing inside her – it left her. It's free.'

'I didn't know.' Denning was thrown.

'Perhaps Philippa has helped to establish a new generation,' Hugo suggested tentatively.

'To watch over us?' Denning sounded sceptical.

'Maybe they believe mankind is too self-destructive to be left entirely to its own devices.'

'And yet they provide this lethal gas? It just doesn't make sense.'

'The Christian God provided the H-bomb.'

'He didn't pass across a formula.'

'The Atlanteans could have changed their minds – or acquired a shred of morality – or even seen some potential in mankind. Perhaps that's why they impregnated her.' Hugo sought for some kind of logic. Could they have seen the possibility of regeneration? Of a new age? Perhaps that was why the Atlanteans had given Denning the knowledge and the power to cancel the formula. 'Your son,' continued Hugo. 'Are you close?'

'Yes.'

'Is he sharing the visions still?'

'I think so. But Garry is terminally ill.'

'What's the matter with him?'

'He's got Aids,' said Denning hurriedly, angrily. 'He had a drug habit but did a cold turkey, had therapy – got himself together again. That was some years ago. Then he was diagnosed HIV positive. Garry contracted full-blown Aids this year and he's dying.'

'How terrible – ' But Hugo had had a sudden and shattering idea which he blurted out without thinking of its effect on Denning. 'Would anyone in Basra make a surprise personal sacrifice?' he said.

[169]

'I don't understand.'

'I – I've been reminding myself of the Islamic terrorists of a few years ago. The men and women who believed so implicitly in their cause that they packed themselves with explosives – and detonated on their target.'

Denning shrugged. 'There aren't any fanatics here.'

'If I didn't have to go back to the pyramid I'd do it myself. I'd wire myself up and walk into that lab and blow it sky high.'

There was a short silence. Finally Denning took the point.

'I can't bear not to be with Garry, to be here in Egypt when he's so ill in the States. I'm sure you feel the same about Brent.'

Hugo nodded with weary impatience. Brent was dead already. He seemed to have forgotten that. The conversation was clearly going nowhere. He had to leave.

'Of course I know I shall be reunited with him in death,' Denning said unexpectedly, walking to the window and looking out on to the alley below. 'I love these people,' he muttered. 'More than I've loved anyone – except Garry.' He turned back to Hugo. 'Do you believe in being reunited with Brent?' He swept on without waiting for a reply. 'Garry has a few weeks to live. A couple of months at the most, so the decision is made.'

'What are you saying?' asked Hugo. Was he going to go ahead?

'Perhaps I was in Atlantis once – maybe Garry, too. I'm a coward, I'm afraid. A terrible coward. But I'm prepared to make the sacrifice although I don't want to take any of these people with me – but I know that I'll have to.'

Hugo looked at Christopher Denning with considerable respect. Now there was a possible future.

'I would have liked to evacuate the people here but it's impossible,' he repeated. 'They'll be the usual innocent victims.'

Hugo saw Denning's despair and it deeply moved him. But there was nothing he could say that would in any way alleviate his grim responsibility. 'The problem is that the Atlanteans could easily replace the formula, and they will if I can't release them.'

'You *have* to release them. But there's something else,' said Denning. 'Something I'm hoping you'll do for me.'

Hugo nodded.

'I'm going to ask you to do me a favour, Mr Fitzroy. I want you to go to Boston. No one else can tell Garry why I did what I'm going to do. I mean, it would never be believed – except by a few. A very few.'

'My son was put in a psychiatric hospital because he wrote the truth.'

'I think we both realize that this secret is much better kept than broadcast,' Denning reminded him gently. 'Will you take the note to Garry?'

'Of course I will.'

'What were you going to do when you release the gods?'

'If I succeed I was – anyway, it doesn't matter. I promise I'll go to him.' Hugo did not want to tell Denning that he had hoped the gods would take him with them.

As Denning wrote to his son, Hugo watched what was happening in the narrow passageway below. A child played with a cat, an old woman sat on a step, a couple of young boys kicked a football at each other and a girl of about eighteen walked up the alley slowly. She was dressed in bedouin style but had a transistor radio in her hand and was singing along to its thumping beat. She danced a few steps, the old woman waved a fist, the cat ran away, the two boys dropped their football. The sharp moonlight lit them like pale, grey ghosts and then the girl and her transistor hurried on, the booming sound diminishing into the night. The boys casually returned to their game, the old lady to her step and the cat to her playmate. The words of the nursery rhyme flooded into Hugo's mind.

> Boys and girls come out to play,
> The moon doth shine as bright as day.
> Leave your supper and leave your sleep,
> And join your playfellows in the street.
> Come with a whoop and come with a call,
> Come with a good will or not at all.

[171]

But they all came with a good will, didn't they, thought Hugo. None of them knew what was going to happen; none of them were in charge of their own fate – and soon they were going to be blown to pieces.

Denning gave the note to Hugo, his face grey with fatigue and trepidation. 'Fill up the jeep with diesel. I shan't go into the lab until I know you're clear. I'm afraid the explosion will have to be very substantial to ensure the right level of destruction. There will be a large number of casualties.'

Hugo realized his old detachment had vanished for ever.

'I'll need some ammunition,' he said abruptly. 'I've no doubt the pyramid will be surrounded with Iraqi troops when I get back.' He suddenly felt defeated, his sense of purpose gone. 'I might as well take as many of the bastards out as I can, but how I'm going to get back into that pyramid and – '

'Wait.' Denning was calm and positive. 'You're not thinking straight. Do you really imagine for one moment the Egyptian government would allow any Iraqi presence around that pyramid? There'll be a few security men, but I'm afraid you're going to have to put your faith in the gods – as I have to. They've guided you before. Surely they'll do it again in their greatest need.'

'I promise you I'll find your son.' Hugo was ashamed of his outburst now. Was it exhaustion that had made him so spineless, he wondered, or was it a reversion to what he had been. I must have changed, thought Hugo. The gods have guided me.

'Will you help Garry?' asked Denning, his agitation showing at last.

'Yes.' Hugo put the note in his wallet. 'You've got to trust.'

They embraced, and in the embrace he felt, for the first time in many decades, a trace of self-respect.

As Hugo drove away, Denning stood by the diesel pump, giving a half wave. Then he began to walk slowly and casually away, hands in pockets, taking his last journey to the laboratory. Hugo imagined him strolling amongst his colleagues, his body as lethal as the formula for the gas they were about to prepare. Perhaps, before the device exploded, he would have time to joke with his colleagues, to answer a question, examine a piece of apparatus. Hugo remembered the fragments of human life that he had photographed in the bar in Belfast. Declan's. Would someone come and photograph the remains in Nazra? Not just the victims in the lab but those, more innocent, sprawled outside in the street, blown to bits. Would the boy in the water survive? Hugo prayed he would. The child had been part of a succession – perhaps would be again. All those lost, deserted children.

He looked at his watch and began to concentrate on what he would have to face. Just after 2 a.m. and he had hours to drive. Suppose he broke down? Suppose they came looking for him? What about an ambush? There were numerous possibilities. Then a new conviction slowly filled him, keeping the creeping panic at bay. He was an Atlantean and so were Philippa and Brent. He was one of the gods.

As he drove back, the sand on the road bleaching out in the headlights below him, Hugo became increasingly oppressed and his elation died. Then the sand-hills began to move and suddenly, without warning, he was in a primeval ocean, at first dun-coloured and then as black as pitch.

'Can we trust you?' The words rang above the lashing waves.

'You know who I am.'

'We needed three. Two are dead.'

'Killed by your false friends.'

'We must leave.'

'You are responsible for their deaths.'

'We don't understand mankind. You seem successful in killing each other and for that reason you have not developed into higher beings. Sometimes you are strong, sometimes so weak. You confuse us. We are concerned only with regeneration.'

'You should have been concerned with understanding. You understand nothing.'

The voices inside him became silent and Hugo lost his temper, crying aloud, 'You won't be watching over anyone, will you? You're false gods.'

At once, the elements around him intensified, the jeep ran off

[173]

the road and Hugo slumped at the wheel. In his mind he was on a ship, running before the wind, the masts bare of sail, sweeping through a sea canyon, with lashing spume on either side and stalagmite-like rocks piercing the water. Dark waves thundered on a primeval shoreline where land crabs crawled towards volcanic gullies and Atlantean globes rose in a leprous sky.

Hugo was in the wheel-house, standing beside Brent who was steering the craft through the treacherous channel which gradually grew narrower. Great gobbets of water, rebounding from the craggy shore, hurled themselves over the deck and in the vast swirl he saw dozens of small fish floating, each with a sorrowful eye watching him.

He was conscious of Philippa's hand in his, of Brent's voice encouraging him, but she was as cold as death and he could see the bones in his son's arm.

The dim light at the end of the channel came up slowly and then, suddenly, with surprising speed as the ship cleaved the dark waves, shrugged off the backlash from the rocky shore and steered between the jagged pinnacles. The light became hazy, but as it cleared he saw Tiderace with the pyramid glowing on the cliffs in the sparkling morning sun. Sea birds called and wheeled and, as they surged nearer, he saw the wall of sand on the beach, battling to hold off the tide.

'You must use the love you lost on the island,' said the voice in his mind, and Hugo knew more clearly what he had to do when he reached Giza.

The noise of the elements was cut off instantly, and somewhat dazed by the silence he found himself no longer in the wheel-house of the ship but behind the wheel of the jeep.

The noise of the explosion was slight but he knew from the distant rumbling that Christopher Denning had sacrificed himself and others.

'You were wrong,' Hugo shouted to the Atlanteans as the sound spread thin and died away.

'Yes.' The answer was almost lost in the scudding breeze. 'We were wrong.'

12

THE PORTAL

The road was undulating over sand-hills again and the wan moonlight turned every dip into a dark hollow. Hugo was struggling to concentrate on the road, but as he plunged the jeep into yet another fold of the dunes he prayed aloud, not just for the great sacrifice that had been made by Christopher Denning but for all the unsuspecting people he had taken with him. He also prayed that he could have enough faith to make this final journey to the pyramid. He prayed to the Christian God but also directed his prayers to all forms and faces of the deity. Because he was so preoccupied, Hugo only just saw the Mercedes half-way across the road with the nearside tyre punctured. He drew the jeep to a screaming halt just in time to avoid a collision, but when he switched off the ignition the silence seemed to grow into a wall around him.

Hugo clambered out, pausing to survey the limousine. There was no one at the wheel, but surely its owner couldn't have wandered off into the desert. Then he caught sight of the huddled form on the rear seat.

Slowly he approached, pacing himself, still not able to see properly. He paused, walked a few more steps, staring ahead, poised, ready for an ambush, the revolver in his hand. There was still no sign of life and he moved closer to gaze in at the rear of the Mercedes. For a while he felt unable to make a decision. Then he pulled open the back door with considerable force and dragged away a couple of old and stinking bedouin blankets. Tarik Ibrahim was lying on the seat, a knife in his hand. His eyes were open but his breathing was laboured. Hugo stared at him in horror. Ibrahim's face was a mask of dried blood, his features black and purple. He looked clownish, ludicrous, but there was a shred of dignity in his eyes.

'Hugo.' Ibrahim's voice gravelled dry as a husk. 'I came to kill you, but I'm dying.' He began to cough and the sound was harsh and grating. Then it became a rattle.

'What can I do?' asked Hugo.

There was silence. Then he said slowly and wonderingly:

'Can you see what I see?'

Spring had come to the cliffs of Tiderace and a little sea breeze trickled through the salt-ridden grass. Brent was there, arms folded, grinning. Philippa emerged from the pyramid with a football in her hand and they began to kick it to and fro just as the boys in Nazra had done.

As the vision faded, Ibrahim said, 'I still believe in Islam.'

'What kind of Islam?'

'The most fundamental. The most pure. What else?'

'Did you really want to be responsible for the use of that chemical warfare – against so many?'

'They are enemies of the faith.'

'Surely you realized that you couldn't release the gods – you and your kind?'

'Yes. But I believed the light walkers would come. And you did.'

'You believed in manipulating us – letting us find the change in frequency – and then destroying her.'

The dreadful rattling cough came again. 'I thought our faith would be strong enough. One day it will be. I have a favour to ask you before you go to the pyramid.'

'What is it?'

'Did you take my revolver?'

'Yes.'

'I imagine you found some ammunition in Nazra?'

Hugo nodded. He knew what Ibrahim wanted him to do.

[176]

'Will you put me out of my pain? You're not taking my life. You're giving me the next.'

Hugo took out the weapon. He held it to Ibrahim's head but felt unable to pull the trigger.

'Please.'

'I can't.'

'Find the strength. Build the strength.'

But his finger would not move.

'Pray with me,' whispered Ibrahim.

'Don't ask me to do that.'

'You *must* pray with me.' Again the rattle.

'How?'

'Repeat these words and on the last you must fire. The final phrase is "And God is not unmindful of what ye do." Do you understand?'

'Yes.'

'Very well.' Slowly and painfully Ibrahim began to pray. 'From whencesoever thou startest forth, turn thy face in the direction of the Sacred Mosque; that is indeed the truth from thy Lord. And God is not unmindful of what you do.'

Hugo pulled the trigger.

The pale dawn slowly streaked the night sky and he could see the shadowed pyramid. He had twenty minutes to go as he brought the jeep to a halt, got out and began to walk over the dunes, the gun in his hand, shaking so much that he could hardly put one foot in front of the other, all too well aware of time darting past at incredible speed.

Glancing frantically at his watch, Hugo began a stumbling run that became a sprint. His breath was coming in panting gasps and a stitch developed in his side. With each step he took the agony increased until there were tears in his eyes and he was sobbing with the sustained effort. Just under fifteen minutes remained now, and although Hugo was nearing the pyramid, he knew that he would encounter opposition. He was therefore hardly surprised when he saw the figure indistinctly in a dip between the dunes, a hump in the sand, lying still. Was he waiting for him? Why hadn't he seen him? Hugo knew he was all too obviously silhouetted on the skyline, but it was no good being cautious, he had to continue, the time swarming away from him like the flies that had guided him to Basra.

Hugo paused, waiting, watching, but there was no movement, no challenge, no warning, and he forced himself on, anticipating any moment the hail of bullets that would cut him down. Wave after wave of despair swept over him, saturating his mind with the inescapable knowledge that if the gods were not released, he would never see Philippa and Brent again. There would be no other lives, and even if he survived he would be trapped on this brutish planet for ever, back in his old rut, photographing Sodom and Gomorrah.

The figure remained motionless and Hugo continued relentlessly to draw nearer, only to discover the man's stillness was the stillness of death; his throat had been cut.

Bemused, Hugo hurried on, speeding up as the panic surged again and again, his chest heaving, his breath coming in gasps, the pain in his side increasing every second. He had so little time left and yet the pyramid was still at least a hundred yards away.

He saw another corpse lying in the dunes, this time on his back with the gash across his throat more visible. Were they all dead? Who had killed them?

Somehow Hugo redoubled his efforts, crying aloud with the agony of the stitch that had begun to pierce rather than to throb. He had under ten minutes left now, but was almost at the door of the pyramid, the sweat running into his eyes, all too conscious of the sun about to rise behind him. Shadows shortened, light grew, then he saw Jamal standing by the pyramid, waiting for him, his hooded eyes sightlessly searching the creeping dawn.

Hugo slowed down, clumsily pulling out the gun, gasping for breath.

[178]

'Let me through.'

But again there was no opposition and Jamal threw open the door of the pyramid. 'I've been waiting for you.'

'Who killed them?'

'Ibrahim. We have both changed our minds. You are blessed, Hugo Fitzroy. Use all your strength and faith and you will release the gods. Your journey won't be in vain.'

He led Hugo by the hand into the grey light of the interior of the pyramid and his touch was warm and comforting. The casket was in the middle of the floor and the silence was absolute. Philippa's corpse was no longer there.

'What do I do?' asked Hugo, panic almost suffocating him.

'Look back to where it began. For you. Put back what you stole.'

'The love.' Hugo squatted down by the casket as light began to seep from the portal. He thought of the sacrifices that had already been made. Brent's, Philippa's, Christopher's. Please God, let it be soon. He closed his eyes and found himself standing on the short green grass of the Tiderace cliffs. The sea below was crested by white horses. The pyramid soared above him and he went inside yet again. Thoth stood in the beam with Isis. Brent and Philippa.

'Will you be here next year, Dad? And the year after next?'

'I'll be with you for ever, Son.' He kissed Brent's cold cheek. 'I'm sorry,' he whispered. 'I'm so very sorry.'

The child is father to the man: the words beat in Hugo's mind.

'The portal's opening,' said Brent's distant voice, and then Hugo was back in the pyramid in the desert, standing in the beam alone with the casket. The light was almost blinding and the dawn sky above was pale gold. Hugo felt consumed by joyous relief as the globes hovered beside him, sharing the moment, and then began to ascend.

He watched them until they were lost to sight in the celestial blue. Then, weeping with happiness and a soaring sense of achievement, he knelt in prayer, not knowing what kind of God –

[179]

or gods – he was praying to but overwhelmed with the ecstasy of sheer release.

The beam disappeared abruptly, and Hugo was alone with Jamal. When he looked down at the casket he could see that it was empty; even the remains of the dead Atlantean had disappeared.

'Where are you going?' he asked.

'Into the desert.'

'Do you know which way to go?'

'I know which way.' Jamal embraced him.

They clung to each other and then walked out into the dawn together. The golden hue of clouds and sky was giving way to the first rays of the sun which crept along the desert floor like fingers searching out a lover. Slowly the cloaked dunes came alive and the light floated on them, turning them amber. Hugo looked up again to the sky but the globes had disappeared.

Jamal touched his shoulder with a withered, sand-grey hand. 'I sense that one remains,' he said.

Sure enough, Hugo could see the small globe. Philippa's child, hovering, watching, waiting.

Hugo walked slowly to the doorway and took one last look inside the pyramid. Would he ever come here again? Would the baby in the globe become a new god? He would have liked to have gone into the desert with Jamal, but he knew he had unfinished business that would take some time.

He remembered Philippa's words: 'If only we could be together for a while in some remote place.'

And he spoke to her again now: 'Not for a while – but for ever.'

He returned outside to see Jamal crouched over a fire. He watched the smoke ascending and knew instinctively that this was Philippa's funeral pyre and he was watching her release too. Soon she would be amongst the gods.

EPILOGUE
Boston

Hugo began his own journal on the plane, trying to record events as they had happened, but his task was difficult and painful. The explosion at Nazra had been widely reported by the world's media – as had his own involvement. Putting down his pen with relief, he picked up the free broadsheet which on this flight was *The New York Herald Tribune* and began to read as if he was learning about a stranger.

INTERNATIONAL PHOTOGRAPHER FLEES BASRA BOMB
Hugo Fitzroy, the distinguished and award-winning international press photographer, escaped from the small Egyptian desert village of Nazra minutes before it was wrecked by a gigantic explosion. Dozens are feared killed, but the emergency services have not yet been able to give the exact number of casualties. The Egyptian government has ordered an immediate inquiry.

This is the third drama in as many months for Fitzroy, who was first knee-capped by an IRA terrorist and later taken hostage by the Iraqis in the Gulf War and held as part of the human shield in an aircraft factory. Escaping from there, he reached the Iran border and was hospitalized in a private clinic. This extraordinary chain of events underlines how hazardous are the lives of those who cover international assignments.

[181]

Mr Fitzroy told me: 'I have no intention of continuing my career as a photographer now. It's time to quit – the Furies have warned me.'

Don Robinson, Picture Editor of the British *Sunday Times*, commented that 'Hugo Fitzroy is probably one of the greatest photojournalists it has ever been my privilege to know. His work is widely recognized and widely exhibited, but what is not so well known is Fitzroy's unique brand of courage. Apart from the obvious risk-taking of his profession, he has always been determined to cover the inside story – and it is the insiders who have proved so dangerous. We are devastated that he has decided to retire but also realize, as Hugo Fitzroy realizes, that he cannot tempt fate again. I understand he is to receive the OBE for services to journalism.'

Lucy had phoned him at the hotel the previous night. She had been sad and reflective, speaking to him self-consciously, as if he had become a stranger.

'I've tracked you down at last. Are you recovering?'

'They say I'm comfortable.'

'How long is all this going on for?'

'Haven't you seen the papers? I'm retiring.'

'You've said that before.' She was doubtful rather than caustic.

'I mean it this time.'

'Hugo – I'm very sorry about Philippa Neville. I saw it was written up as a separate paragraph. Easy to miss.'

'They've connected the two stories,' Hugo had replied. 'But everything is pending an inquiry and there's a somewhat belated news blackout.'

'Anyway – I'm sorry,' she had repeated bleakly.

'Thank you.'

'What will you do when you're better?'

'Fly to Boston.'

'An assignment?' She had sounded cynical but had managed to laugh.

'I'm going to give someone a message.'

'And then?'

'I'll hang up my camera.'

There had been an awkward silence. Then she had said, 'I believe you will, this time.'

'I thought I'd get a house that has a view of the island.' But he only said that to comfort her.

They had talked for another ten minutes until Lucy sprang her shock card. 'I'll come back to you. If you want me to. We could make a fresh start.'

'Have you broken with Tim?' Hugo was surprised, and acutely aware she was just part of the distant past. But he did not want to hurt her; he had done enough of that already.

'No,' she admitted.

'So it's to be bigamy?' he asked lightly.

'I *love* you, Hugo. Do you love me?'

'You know how fond – ' he began.

'So it *was* Philippa.'

'Yes.'

'I'm still prepared to come back and – '

'Look after me?'

'Begin again.'

'No. It's too late for that. My fault.'

'You'll promise me one thing, though?' she had said reluctantly.

'What's that?'

'We can meet. Be friends.'

'Of course we can,' he had reassured her, conscious even as he said it that soon, hopefully, he would no longer be around.

Now Hugo lay back exhausted in his seat, praying that directly he returned from Boston the gods would repay him. He shivered, the flow of air-conditioning chilling him to the bone. Suppose they didn't?

The clapboard house was in the country, and had an air of quiet elegance. The rye grass was trimly mowed, the sprinkler moved in graceful arcs, the rose trellis, the manicured flower beds, the Buick in the drive, the bike – the American dream that Hugo had once found enticing with its rigid sense of identity and affluence.

[183]

As he stood and watched, a boy came out of the house wearing a turned-round baseball cap on his head. He thought he had Brent's eyes.

'Hi.'

'I'm Hugo Fitzroy. Your mother's expecting me.'

'You come to see Garry?'

'Yes. How is he today?'

'Not so good.'

He followed the boy into the sweet-scented pine hallway, and a woman with swept-back hair and a heavily lined face came out of the kitchen.

'You're Christopher's friend.' They shook hands and Hugo felt her anxiety as she came straight to the point. He liked her for that.

'No one will tell me why he was in that dreadful place. He used to work in Cairo. That's when I was with him.' She paused and muttered, 'But I shouldn't have left Garry alone.' She turned to the boy. 'You have papers to deliver.' She smiled, taking the sting out of the words. 'Get going, Sean.'

He slouched out and she turned back to Hugo. 'I'm Elaine Denning – of course, you'd know that. You'll have to forgive me – I'm not very together these days. What with Chris and Garry.'

'Chris was working on a government project – to do with germ warfare. Someone sabotaged the lab.'

'Had you spent much time with him?' She was anxious for more detail.

'Just a few hours.'

'You must have got friendly for him to ask you to take a note to Garry.' She looked at him rather absently.

'We hit it off.'

'Did he have some – presentiment?'

'Maybe. There'd been warnings,' Hugo improvised.

'So you'll want to see my son?'

'If I may.'

'He's not having a good day, so please don't stay with him too long.' Hugo was about to assure her that he would not when she added sadly, 'He's very near death now.' She laughed absently. 'The grim reaper seems to be continually hovering just outside

[184]

his bedroom door. I keep falling over his scythe.' She laughed again, and then gave a half-sob.

'I'm so sorry – '

'We know that because he keeps hallucinating – says he can see a pyramid.' Hugo nodded. He had been expecting that.

'Garry?'

The face on the pillow was chalk white. He must be in his early twenties, thought Hugo, but acknowledged the possibility of his being younger. The eyes were enormous, sunk into their sockets, and his hair was lank, lifeless, a thatch of brown straw.

'You Dad's friend?' His voice was weak, but not listless.

'Yes.' There was a particular smell in the room – chemical, sweet, slightly fetid. 'I've got a letter for you.'

Garry took the note in his thin, claw-like hands and spent some time reading. 'You seen this?' he asked eventually.

'No.'

'Must have been a temptation.'

'One I resisted.'

'Shall I read it to you?'

'Only if you want to.'

' "The bearer of this note is Hermes, son of Thoth. He has released the gods. Soon he will release you. Believe me, the Atlanteans were desperate enough to trade evil, but their progeny will not make such compromises. Can mortals undo what the gods have done? At least Hugo Fitzroy and I made the final sacrifice." '

'I don't have long,' said Garry. 'But what will you do?'

'Take a boat out to Tiderace.'

'In the hope they'll come back for you there?'

'Something like that.'

'Would you consider taking me with you?'

Hugo looked startled. 'I can't do that.' He began to search for reasons.

'Why not?'

'Your mother would never allow you to travel. Neither would your doctor.'

[185]

'I could say that Dad thought the island was a centre of healing. I mean – the medics can't do anything for me, can they?' His voice was stronger and his sunken eyes gleamed with a hope that Hugo knew he couldn't snuff out.

'Would she accept that?'

'She had the highest regard for Dad's intuition. That was about the only thing they had going for them.'

'You're so frail.' Hugo knew, however, that he would take him.

'So is the seed – the new god. I had this weird dream – only last night. I was on a cliff top and a beam of light came in from over the sea and I kind of bathed in it. Later on I walked back to the beach and there you were, playing with your kid.'

'What happened next?'

'I don't know. It hasn't happened yet.' Garry was bolt upright, his hands reaching out, his eyes shining. Hugo knew that he had as much to offer to this sick boy as the gods had to offer to him.

'I'll go down and see your mother,' said Hugo.

'Please, God – make her understand.'

Garry was so weak that the walk up the cliff path was too much and several times Hugo had to half carry him. He was almost unconscious when they reached the top, where the weather was misty and dull, the sea moving sluggishly below. He wrapped his coat around the boy's thin frame.

'They'll come,' he said, with confidence.

They sat on the salt grass for an hour while the mist thickened, but at no time did Hugo's faith weaken. He put his arms around Garry's shoulders and held him tight. They did not speak for a long time, simply watching the mist slowly rise and the sun spread halting rays over the grey ocean.

'Will they come?' whispered Garry.

'Oh yes,' replied Hugo with complete assurance. 'They'll come.'

Gradually the waves turned a crystal green and the damask light spread. A gull wheeled over their heads, seeming to mock them with its plaintive cries, and somewhere from the horizon came a hollow booming.

'Shall we pray?' asked Garry.

The beam came out of nowhere, bathing them in its radiance.